A PLACE IN THE
Promised
Land

A PLACE IN THE
Promised Land

Darlene Hoven

Scythe Publications, Inc.
A Division of Winston-Derek Publishers Group, Inc.

PUBLISHED BY SCYTHE PUBLICATIONS, INC.
Nashville, Tennessee 37205

Library of Congress Catalog Card No: 96-60197
ISBN: 1-55523-797-5

Printed in the United States of America

To Heather Druliner, Jason Shilling,
Ann Marie Klein, Amanda Klein,
Jamie Joleen Klein, Matthew Klein,
Ryan De Joode, Joshua Klein,
Kari Marie De Joode, and little
Gerrit Jacob Klein.
May this book inspire you and teach you
a little of your heritage and culture.
Love, Grandma

Chapter One:
The Secret

"Sarah! Sarah Rose Spoolstra, wake up and help me!"

I knew the voice was that of my sister-in-law, Beatrice. But I wanted to stay abed to contemplate the problem that had been bothering me. I knew something was wrong when my brother Jan went missing for three sunny days in March when it was time to plow the soil for spring planting. Then Pa sold some of the horses and cows, including Jan's favorite horse. Even I knew that you were supposed to sell animals in the fall, not in the spring before the calves and colts were born. Besides, you needed the horses to plow the soil. Jan had disappeared before. He went to Leerdam in July of 1846 and was gone again to Utrecht in December of 1846. He even missed spending Christmas with us.

My family thought that a girl of twelve was not old enough to know what was going on in the world. My eldest brother, Teunis, and his wife, Beatrice, thought if *kindren* heard no evil and saw no evil, they would do no evil. They wanted me to be an innocent young maiden.

I wanted to know things and go places and think for myself. Sometimes I was quiet. I stayed in the corner and kept out of sight. I hoped they would forget that I was in the room. I over-heard enough to know that Jan was meeting with other church people to form a new church. He thought that religion and politics should be separate.

Jan did not like what he called the "ritualistic authority" of the state church. Our older brother, Teunis, and Teunis's wife Beatrice, did not agree. They said that Jan should mind his own business and let God do the judging.

I overheard parts of these conversations for years. Ma never worried much about what I heard. But now she was dead.

Teunis and Beatrice and their two boys, Cornelus and Nicholaas, had moved in with Pa and me. Beatrice kept her eye on me. She seemed to want to know what I was doing every minute.

But something new was about to happen. I could almost feel it in the air. I had to know what was going on. Jan looked happy one minute and sad the next minute. Pa, on the other hand, was always sad these days. I never saw him smile anymore, not since last November when Ma took sick and died. But this was different. Now, whenever he looked at Jan, Pa quickly looked away, and I often saw a tear slide down into the fold of his wrinkled cheek. I never saw Pa cry before Ma died.

I had to know what was going on. When I asked, Beatrice just said, "Why, Sarah, I do not know what you are talking about." I told her that something was going on with Jan, but she just said he was meeting with bad people who did not obey the government. "If he does not watch out, Jan may be put into prison—"

"But Jan wouldn't do anything wrong!" I interrupted her.

Beatrice said, "There is a law that dissenters, like your brother, can not meet in groups of more than nineteen people. Ya, Jan could be fined or put into prison. Now, just be a good girl, and do not worry your pretty head about it. Peel these potatoes. Obey your father and me and your country. Do you have to be so messy? You must know that cleanliness is next to Godliness? I just wish your mother had taught you how to do

2

more household chores. She shouldn't have let you run off to old Hendrika's house. I do not think that the books she loans you are fit for a child to read. I—"

"Don't talk about my mother like that!" I cried. I ran out of the kitchen, slamming the door.

Now I *had* to find out what was going on. I decided to sneak into the parlor and hide and listen. I knew that Beatrice would serve tea at precisely four o'clock, because Beatrice was always punctual. I decided to crawl behind the little table in the corner that held the lamp. It had a long tablecloth that hung to the floor and would cover me.

It wasn't long before Beatrice and Jan's new wife, Mary, and Mrs. Antje de Jong were seated upon the overstuffed chairs. Beatrice poured the tea, holding out her little finger in that proper way of hers.

"Antje, have you met my new sister-in-law, Mary Spoolstra?" Beatrice asked.

"You aren't Roman Catholic? Are you?" Mrs. de Jong asked.

"Goodness gracious, no," said Beatrice. "Mary believes with Jan that the church is corrupt, and she is going with Jan to America with a group led by that jailbird, Dominie Scholte," Beatrice burst out.

To America! Jan and Mary were going to America? I was so excited that I almost jumped up. Instead, I held my breath and peeked out to see what was going on. Mary's face was beet red, although her normal complexion was quite rosy. "No offense intended, dear," Mrs. de Jong said. "It is just that Mary is such a common name for a Roman Catholic. My husband and I have talked about leaving in April, since his pa and brother are leaving Friesland to go to Amsterdam. They will sail on the *Pieter Floris* to Baltimore in the United States of America."

Mary responded, "That is the ship that Jan and I will sail on."

Antje said, "I just can not leave my Ma and sisters. Pieter says if I am not willing to go and suffer the inconveniences and the heartache of leaving, he will not go either."

3

"Ha!" Beatrice laughed. "'Inconvenience' is a pretty mild word for the trip that Jan has in mind! They will be lucky if they do not drown in a storm at sea. All that tossing and rolling on a ship is not for me. They don't even know where they will settle after they arrive in Baltimore."

Mary looked the other two women in the eye and said, "I believe that a woman should go with her husband. Like Ruth in the Bible, I say, 'Entreat me not to leave thee, or to return from following after thee: for whither thou goest, I will go; and where thou lodgest, I will lodge: thy people shall be my people, and thy God my God: where thou diest, will I die, and there will I be buried.'"

There was silence in the room for a minute. Then the clock struck five. Beatrice stood up. That was the signal for company to leave. Tea time was over.

Beatrice and Mary escorted Mrs. de Jong to the door.

Beatrice picked up Ma's blue delft cups and saucers.

Mary returned to the parlor. Softly she said, "Sarah, I know you're behind the table. Come home with me."

I walked with her to the little two-room cabin that was attached to the barn.

"Why wouldn't anyone tell me what's going on?" I asked.

"This family has its secrets," agreed Mary. "They may feel you are too young to understand the significance of the religious problem. Do you realize that Jan could be fined or even put into prison for his beliefs? No one knows what the politie will do if they learn of so many Dutch people leaving this country. The politie may arrest all the men or take all the food and our household goods that we need to survive the trip to America. Also, no one wants you to be upset about our leaving you behind. You may never see us again! These are the reasons why you were not told about the trip."

"I am going to miss Jan, and of course, you and the baby too," I cried. "That is why Pa is so sad." Mary nodded her head.

Now I understood a little more of what was happening. This

4

was not a grand adventure but a life threatening and life changing event!

Mary sighed and said, "I may as well tell you the rest of it. Teunis wants more room for his family. He wants you and Pa to move into the cabin after we leave. He is the eldest son and will inherit the farm, you know."

Of course I knew. I grew up with the idea of primogeniture, where only the firstborn male inherited the land. It was thought that if the farm were divided into land for several sons, then none would have enough ground to survive. That is why Jan had been sent to the University at Leyden. He was expected to earn his living through his education.

"But Pa is still alive! It isn't fair! I get so mad when Beatrice uses Ma's things! What about me? Don't I have any say in any of this? I get so tired of being told that I'm just a child!"

"Well, when you do housework for Pa, you won't be just a child anymore. Pa is blessed to have a daughter to care for him in his old age." If Mary thought that would make me feel better, it wasn't working. I did not like it. I didn't like it one little bit!

Chapter Two:
The Trunks

April 3, 1847 was my thirteenth birthday. No one paid much attention to me. No one even baked me a cake. Mary was planning to, but she was too sick that day. I guess it was just the excitement of leaving her family—and us, too, of course.

They were all busy packing Jan and Mary's belongings into large wooden trunks with strange carvings on the lids. The trunks were huge. They were four to five feet long and about three feet wide, with curved, raised tops. I thought they looked like treasure chests in the books about pirates that Hendrika loaned me.

The family was sorting everything out. Of course, all of Ma's belongings, especially the parlor things, would not fit into the little cabin attached to the barn. Jan and Mary planned to take a few of the things with them, but Beatrice would receive most of what was left. Nothing special was saved for me. The little bed in the cupboard-like corner of the cabin's sitting room would be Pa's, and I would sleep on a cot in the kitchen. I wouldn't even have my own room anymore. Beatrice told Pa that of course we could come to the big house for special occasions such as holidays. Pa simply nodded and didn't say anything. It just wasn't fair!

Since I was now thirteen, I looked in the mirror to see if there were any physical change in me. I was disappointed. There wasn't anything special about me. The only thing round on me was my face. I had blue eyes and brown hair that hung down in two braids. I wasn't very tall, but I was skinny, so when Jan wanted to tease me, he called me the runt of the family.

I had been very special to Ma. She said that she had always prayed for a little girl. She said that even though she had to wait a long time, I was the daughter she had always hoped for. If Ma were alive, I would have had a birthday cake.

I went for a walk along the dikes and canal, and I cried.

There were four ships sailing for America in April of 1847. Their names were the *Pieter Floris*, the *Nagasaki*, the *Catherine Jackson*, and the *Maastroom*. Jan and Mary and their baby, little Jan, were going to sail on the *Pieter Floris*.

I overheard the plans that Beatrice had made for her sons and me. Cornelus and Nicholaas were to stay overnight for a few nights with the de Jong family. She convinced Antje de Jong that I would come along to take care of the boys. Beatrice and Teunis and Pa would then accompany Mary and Jan to the ship. But I didn't want to be left behind! How I longed to see the ships with their sails billowing in the breeze!

When no one was looking, I took a nail that I had gotten from the blacksmith's son. The nails, with their square heads, were valuable because they were all fashioned by the black-smith and required much time and care to make. I wanted to hide in one of the trunks, and I knew that I would need air. So I took the nail and hit it hard with a stone. Sure enough, I made a nice, small hole just under the lid. After that, I made a few more on each end of the trunk.

I was as good as I could be during the next two days. Then we loaded the two trunks into the wagon and hitched up the horses to go to the house of our neighbors, the de Jongs. We arrived there just at nine o'clock, which was coffee time. Several of the other neighbors were there to bid Jan and Mary farewell.

"Jan," I said, "I don't want to cry in front of all these people. Can I just say goodbye now and go for a walk?"

Jan patted my head and said, "Sure, little sister. Be good and study hard. Take care of Pa. I will send you a letter from America. When we get settled in Pella, you can write to me."

Since it was nine o' clock, the adults all went inside the house for coffee and *ole bollen*. I got the de Jong children to show Cornelus and Nicholaas the baby ducklings while I ran to the barn. I took two heavy quilts out of the trunk to make room for me. I hid the quilts under the hay, then crawled into the trunk that was still on the wagon, and I shut the lid. At ten o'clock, coffee time was over. Pa, Teunis, Beatrice, Jan, Mary, and little Jan then proceeded to the ship.

My plan was to reveal my whereabouts when we got to the ship. I figured that they wouldn't be so apt to yell at me if we were in public. Then, too, they would be concerned with their goodbyes. The next thing I knew, however, there was a lot of noise at the dock. Teunis said something about a little gift, and they put heavy locks onto the trunks. My trunk was being hoisted on board with me in it! I tried to yell, but no one heard me.

Chapter Three:
The Stowaway

I must have slept off and on. I was terrified! The trunk felt like a coffin. I was cramped. Something was sticking into my back. I felt the ship sway back and forth with the waves. I tried to yell, but my throat was dry. I was hungry, too. All I had to eat were two peppermints that I had in my pocket. I feared I'd die of hunger or thirst. "Oh, God," I prayed. "Get me out of here, and I'll be good for the rest of my life!"

I slept. I dreamed that I was Jonah in the belly of the great fish!

The next thing I knew was the heavenly sunshine on my face. The light blinded me. I caught a glimpse of my brother's confused but angry face. "Sarah, what are you doing here?" he demanded.

I was crying. "I'm so sorry! I'll be good always! Thank you, thank you for saving me!"

Jan brought Doc De Vries to see me. He scratched his head as he looked me over. "She needs fluids," he announced. "Don't give her too much at a time, though. A little broth will be all right for tonight, and then some thin porridge in the morning.

Give her a little bit at a time." I tried to stand on wobbly legs but couldn't.

"I don't know whether to hug you or spank you!" Jan declared.

"Could you hug me first, and then get me the broth?" I asked tearfully.

"Sweet serendipity Sarah Rose!" Jan tried to be tough with me, but his face showed that he was more likely to tease than to scold. "You are aptly named."

"Just what do you mean by that?" I dared to look him in the eye.

"Sarah means 'princess,' and there is something regal about you, commanding me to bring you food. Serendipity is when someone has a special, magical quality that finds goodness without even looking for it. Serendipity Sarah Rose, you could fall into a pile of manure and come out smelling like a rose!"

Jan brought me to Mary. "What are you doing here, Sarah?" She asked, alarmed.

After sipping some broth, I gave them the details of my escapade. Mary didn't chastise me—she only wanted to know where Jan had put the quilt. I had been saved because she wanted another blanket to put over her seasick body. Since the ship was sailing north by northwest, it was terribly cold.

"I hid two quilts under the hay in the de Jong barn to make room for me," I confessed.

"I forgot the blanket when I saw Sarah," Jan said. "I'll get it for you now."

Only then did I realize how sick Mary and little Jan were. Mary was too sick to do much work. It was all she could do to feed the baby and eat and drink herself. She often vomited her food. I went to the deck whenever possible to breathe the fresh air. The odor of the tar, bilge-water, food, vomit, and sweat was overpowering.

I helped Jan when it was our turn to cook on one of the two stoves in the galley. We were allowed one gallon of fresh water a day per adult and a half gallon per child. Neither Jan nor I was much of a cook. Mary ate the weak tea and the porridge to keep up her strength so she could provide milk for the baby. We also ate salt meat, hardtack, potatoes, and rice.

As the days went by, we met other passengers and everyone worked to help each other. The men lowered buckets on ropes into the sea, and then the women would heat the water to wash our clothes. We were not allowed to use the precious fresh water for this. Of course, the high salt content in the seawater made our washed clothes scratchy and stiff. With the leftover water from the washing, both men and women mopped the decks. The sailors laughed and said that we scrubbed the ship more than any passengers they had ever seen. In fact, their ship would probably never be so clean again. We liked that reputation. We firmly believed that cleanliness was next to Godliness.

The baby weakened. Was the redness on his skin from the harsh washing of his clothes, or was he getting the scarlet fever that Doc said several of the children had? Jan asked the doctor to look at little Jan. He said that Mary's breast milk was the best thing to feed the baby. Doc said to keep washing Jan's little body with the fresh water. Little Jan just made little mewing sounds like a sick kitten now. He didn't even have tears when he cried.

It was four o'clock in the morning on May 4, 1847 when little Jan died. He was only nine months old. I was awakened by Mary's screams and sobs as she held the stiff, cold baby in her arms.

There were two bodies for the funeral that day. Fourteen-year-old Grace De Vries had also died during the night. At seven o'clock the passengers came out on deck. Each of the two bodies was wrapped in a sail filled with stones from the ballast. The first mate placed a plank across a barrel that extended overboard. The De Vries family stood on one side of the plank, and Jan and Mary and I stood with the captain on the other side. The congregation of passengers stood around us. All the men took off their hats and bowed their heads.

The Captain solemnly read Psalm 23. At his signal, sailors stepped up to the plank and placed a body on it. It made an awful splash as it slid into the sea, and then the second body soon followed it. The Dominie, which is what we called our clergyman, announced the singing of Psalm 103, verses 8 through 18. Then he said a prayer.

I don't know how long I stood with my head bowed, but suddenly I felt a touch on my hand. I looked up into the blue eyes of a boy a little older than myself.

"I am sorry," he said.

Chapter Four:
The Ocean Voyage

I saw the same young man again the next night. I had finished washing the pewter dishes we used for our soup and hard bread and tea. The voymester had blown on his pitch pipe and led us in the singing of Psalm 100. The Dominie had finished his prayer. Most of the two hundred Dutchmen and women had gone to tuck their children into their cots or hammocks. I stood alone on the deck.

"Aren't you afraid to be alone?" a voice said behind me.

I jumped and held to the rail as I whirled around to see who had spoken.

It was the same boy I had seen the day before, at the funeral for little Jan and Grace De Vries. He had been so sympathetic. When he spoke to me, I had simply nodded my head to acknowledge that I'd heard him. I had not trusted my voice to speak. Now, however, I straightened my back and shoulders and looked him in the eye.

"No, I am not afraid," I said emphatically. "I'm alone a lot."

"I know what you mean," he said. He seemed embarrassed. "I mean, I know how you feel."

I blinked to keep from crying and stiffened up even more. I wanted to look down on him, but that was impossible since I was only four feet nine inches tall. He was at least a foot taller. "And just how could you know what I feel?" I said reproachfully.

He looked at me as though he were sorry that he'd spoken to me. "I thought we might have many of the same feelings," he said. "Maybe I was wrong."

I looked at the worn wooden deck and said nothing.

He tried again. "I know that even though our loved ones go to be with the Lord, we wonder why. We miss them."

For once, I didn't know what to say. I simply nodded. "Ya, you're right. But it's so hard! Jan's baby seemed to have a whole life ahead of him in the New World. One of the reasons to move to America was to have a better place for little Jan to grow up." I was surprised that I'd revealed so much of my inner thoughts. But he was so easy to talk to, and once I started, I went on and on. It was such a comfort to talk to someone who listened and understood.

The name of my comforter was Pieter De Vries. He was the son of Doc and brother to Grace, the young girl who'd also been buried at sea. Grace had been ill a long time with a heart problem. She was always small for her age, and she'd always been weak. People were always catering to her needs, doing whatever she wanted. Now Mrs. De Vries was blaming her husband, the doctor, for Grace's death. She said that he should have known that Grace did not have the stamina for the sea voyage.

Pieter felt left out. He didn't think that anyone cared about him. They were too busy with their own feelings to pay attention to him. Apparently that was nothing new. Pieter believed that his mother blamed herself for giving birth to an imperfect child, and his father felt guilty because he thought that he should have been able to make Grace well.

What can I say to Pieter? I want to sympathize with him and help him to understand what is happening in his family. If I can

16

not help, at least I can let him know that I will listen. I am so lonely, and I need and friend so badly! If I do not help, will he be a friend to me?

I lay awake in the hammock in the dark, swaying ship. You would think that the gentle motion would put me to sleep, but I had too much on my mind. I was trying to understand how I felt about all that is happening to me, but too many changes were happening in my life so I only felt numb. What must I do to feel like a whole person with a purpose for living? Maybe, if I gathered all the pieces of information about what's happening, I could sort them out and put them into neat little piles. Then I could make sense out of my life. This hollow ache inside of me would go away. I would know the purpose of my life and where I am needed and wanted. My life would be filled with happiness and love.

Who could help me? Mary was too sick. Jan thought of me as a baby sister and would not be serious. He would just tell me not to worry. Maybe Pieter would help me. Then we both could gather information and sort it out. Maybe life would make sense. Maybe I could be happy again.

I fell asleep and dreamed of facts and ideas and dreams that were as concrete as bricks. Pieter and I were laying these bricks into rows and building a road. In my dream, there were children waiting for us to build the road so they could journey on it.

The following day, Pieter found me sitting on the edge of a trunk with my needlework on my lap. I was interlocking looped stitches with a single piece of yard and a hooked needle. I was making a square that could be a dishcloth. Since I kept dropping stitches, it was not very good. Needlework was not my favorite thing to do but I was trying to look industrious.

"Am I interrupting something important?" Pieter queried.

I smiled. "No, I would much rather talk to you."

"Do you like to do needlework?"

"Absolutely not," I answered. "But it is woman's work so I guess I am stuck with it. Pieter, if you could do any kind of work

17

you wanted, what would you do?"

Pieter's face was very serious and he answered, "I would be a doctor. I want to know what makes people sick and what make them well. I want to know how to prevent disease."

I asked, "Would your father like for you to be a doctor?"

"Ya, I think that it would please him. I think that he wants me to follow in his footsteps. But that is alright because I really want to be a doctor. If we knew enough about medicine and the progress of disease, maybe Grace would not have died."

Pieter swallowed as though he was trying to get rid of a lump in his throat and fighting to keep from crying, so I changed the subject.

"I had a dream last night. I was trying to find the meaning of life. I wrote on bricks all the facts of everything that has happened to me in my life. You helped me write down other facts on bricks. Then we took all the bricks and sorted them and built a road." I looked Pieter in the eye to see if he would laugh.

Pieter did not laugh. "That is not a stupid idea," he said.

"But I do not have any bricks," I answered.

Pieter sighed. "I mean let's talk about facts and ideas and dreams and try to sort out their meaning," he said seriously.

"Well, I ah–"

"A well is a deep hole. You can get water from it."

I looked at him again. Was Pieter taking me seriously enough? I decided to challenge him.

"Alright. Tell me why things are happening the way they are. Why are our people separating from the State Church and the Catholic Church?"

Pieter took the challenge. "We separated from the Roman Catholic Church in the 1500s at the time of Reformation under the leadership of such men as John Calvin and Martin Luther. The reformers believed that salvation was achieved through the grace of God and the payment of Jesus Christ on the cross. Therefore, atoning of one's sins through indulgences or absolution was wrong, because every man should be his own priest.

18

Our leaders felt that the teaching of the scriptures and the whole church service should be in our own language and not in Latin. Now, the State Church is too much like the Roman Catholic Church with it's ritualistic, formal services," Pieter paused.

"Have you ever been to a State Church service?" I asked.

"Ya," Pieter continued. "They make the sign of the cross and they kneel a lot. Their responsive reading is more like chanting. They do not use the Heidelberg Catechism as an evangelical statement of faith. But the most important difference between our religion and the Roman Catholics and the State religion, is that we are going to God through prayer and searching the scriptures for ourselves instead of through a priest. We must be active in finding the answers to life–not just accepting the word of someone else."

"You sound like a future preacher, not a doctor." I tried to put a little levity into the conversation.

"You asked for it," Pieter answered. "But I really do not want to study Greek and Hebrew to become a preacher. You know they have to learn to read the Bible in it's original languages. I really want to become a doctor."

"Do you think that I will ever be able to get more education?" I queried.

"You already know how to read and write. That is all you need to teach your children the Bible. You will not earn your own living because you are a girl. Why do your want to learn more?"

I was angry. I jumped from my seat on the trunk, ready to walk away. "You sound just like my brother, Jan. He got to go to the University and learn to be a surveyor. He got to study the fine arts and humanities as well. He was not limited to vocational and technical skills by being an apprentice. He did not learn to be a blacksmith, or cobbler, or cooper or tailor–," I was out of breath from my tirade.

"Sarah, please quiet down. Someone will think that I have done something to hurt you!" Pieter implored.

"Pieter, you hurt my feelings!" I cried.

19

"Sarah I am sorry. I spoke without thinking. You really are serious, aren't you? I never met a girl as serious as you."

"But I want so much to learn and study. Pieter, will you help me? Will you talk to me and teach me? I need to know what is happening so I can make sense of my world. I want... Oh Pieter, will you please come and talk to me again?"

"Sure little friend," Pieter said with a grin. "It will be nice to have someone listen to me for a change."

Chapter Five:
Discussions aboard Ship

Pieter and I met each night when the weather was good and discussed what we had learned during the course of the day. What I liked best was listening to the talk about America. It was easy to hear the men and women talking; there was little privacy anywhere on the ship. Each person had their own place for sleeping below deck, and if they were lucky, it was separated from their neighbor's area by a blanket hung from the rafters. Still, there was no problem hearing what went on all over the ship.

The new town was to be called "Pella." Pella was the name of an ancient city located about twenty-four miles northwest of Thessalonica, Greece. It had been a great city until it was conquered by Rome in 168 B.C. They also said that it was the birthplace of Alexander the Great. Of course, those were not the true reasons to call our American town Pella. They wanted going to call it Pella because it meant the "city of refuge." Here they could worship God as they pleased.

I was surprised that no one knew where this town was to be located. It was hard to imagine eight hundred people making a voyage to the other side of the world without knowing exactly where their destination was. The men wanted to have flat land and thought that the prairies in the middle of America sounded good. A few hills might be all right. They needed water, too, so it would be good to be near a river. A few trees would be nice for timber to build houses, and a few Dutchmen joked about needing the trees for new shoes. Wind for windmills was a necessity for others, and most men agreed that they would not feel at home in the mountains. They wanted a place similar to the wet, low land of the Netherlands. Somehow, some way, God would lead them to a place in this promised land. As the weeks went by and I listened to this talk, I was still not sure where I would fit in.

I wanted to know what the geographical place called Pella would be like. I wanted to know if I would be living on a few acres or in town. Would I ever feel like I belonged to the land? Where was *my* place in this promised land?

Of course, no one agreed on how much land was necessary to support a family. Most settlers declared they needed at least forty acres of farmable land for each man in a family. Some men wanted a section of one hundred sixty acres.

The American government had so much trouble with the paper money issued by individual states that it accepted only gold or silver in the purchase of federal land. So the Dutchmen had sold most of their possessions for the golden coins we called guilders. These guilders were kept in one large iron chest, guarded by two men day and night because it held all the money for the land we were to buy. I never saw them carry the chest, but Pieter said it took six men. Each family kept their own expense money, which they would need for the trip inland once they reached the New World. I didn't want to even think about what would happen if somehow the golden guilders were stolen.

Mary gradually became a little stronger and often walked the deck with me. She met Mrs. De Vries, and although little was said about the deaths of baby Jan and fourteen-year-old Grace, the women seemed drawn together by their common sorrow. They sewed together, and sometimes our families ate together.

Mrs. De Vries also shared some Gouda cheese and raisins with us, so our menu grew a little more varied. I enjoyed the raisins cooked in the rice. Each person provided the food for their own family before boarding the ship. Of course, no provision had been made for me, but I realized we had more food than we had during the first week of our trip. The De Vries family must have given Grace's portion to Jan and Mary for me. I felt a little guilty about that.

Not many people knew how I had arrived on ship. I knew that a proper, well raised young lady just didn't do things like that, and I was relieved to hear no one talking about it.

I worried about what we were going to do when we landed. Jan didn't have any papers for me. Would we be delayed because of the papers? Would we have to wait for the ship to return to the Netherlands and then bring the papers on the next voyage? That would mean waiting at least a year, because the ship wouldn't return until then. Jan would never send me back alone. Would we be separated from the colony while we waited in Baltimore for the papers to arrive? Mary and I spoke no English. And even though Jan spoke only a little English, he had planned to find work assisting with the surveying in the new colony. I worried and prayed and cried about it every night.

When Pieter saw my red eyes, he asked me to tell him what was troubling me. Pieter was a good friend, but what could he do about it? He said that he would speak to his father, but I didn't see what he could do about it, either.

To my surprise, Doc De Vries did come up with a solution— although it proved to be a deceitful one. I would simply become Grace De Vries. Our families would stay together, and Doc would keep the papers for me. Mrs. De Vries gave me Grace's clothes to wear, and although Grace had been a year older than I, the clothes fit quite well because Grace had been so small. I really felt strange. Could I put on a new identity as easily as new clothing?

Land, land! It was mass confusion as people ran to the deck clutching their loved ones for dear life. After almost six weeks at sea, we were happy to see land. Everyone was shouting orders for members of their family. My hands trembled as I nervously changed into Grace's best dress. Soon would be the dreaded moment of inspection. Would I pass inspection?

The American inspectors looked at the papers and changed many names to American versions. They said the Americans could not pronounce or spell the Dutch names. My brother Jan was now John and Pieter became Peter. They pronounced my brother's name with a harsh "J" sound. We had always pronounced it with a "Y" sound. We said "Yon."

I had never been so scared in my entire life! My heart felt like it was in my throat as we stood in a long line to pass inspection. Jan or John and Mary stood by me, along with the De Vries family. Jan said "ya" to the inspector but no one else spoke. I do not think I could talk if I wanted to. I tried to swallow the huge lump in my throat, but my throat was too dry.

The health officers were quite impressed with the cleanliness of the ship. I still thought it smelled funny. They looked us over for signs of tuberculosis or infectious disease. I did not dare look them in the eye. I hoped they would just think that I was shy.

We then queued up in another line where the inspector stamped our papers. "Welcome to America, Grace," he said.

He was speaking to me. "Ya," I answered.

Chapter Six:
The Journey Inland

I'll never forget the sight of garbage in the street in Baltimore. People just opened their windows and poured their slop jars into the street. It stank. I thought that the odors aboard ship were bad! This was definitely worse. Some of the streets were paved with cobblestone or brick, but the streets near the port were mud, pure and simple. Chickens and pigs ran into the streets to forage among the garbage. I saw a filthy woman with black teeth spitting tobacco on the street. I even saw a darkie unloading a ship. I had never seen a black man before. He joined several others like him who were singing a wailing, chanting song, the like of which I had never heard. It was almost a cry. I shivered even though the day was warm.

We were the last of the four ships to dock in Baltimore. The date was June 12, 1847. We were welcomed by the other Dutch people who had sailed on the other three ships. There were about eight hundred of us altogether. For a few days, we took shelter as best we could in whatever we could rent. The people of Maryland were hospitable us, especially when they saw our gold guilders.

The food was one of the best things about arriving on land. Although June 12 was too early for fresh vegetables, rhubarb and strawberries were already available. Aboard ship we weren't able to do much baking because we needed to share the two little stoves with so many families. The threat of a large, log-burning fire getting out of control also impeded baking. Now the women cooked and baked with pleasure. It was also good to wash the salt out of our clothes and hair.

We met with some former neighbors and churchmen that Jan and Mary knew. They told us that there had been deaths on the other ships, too. The Teunis Klein family, who had sailed on the Maastroom, lost three of their four children en route to America. Arie had been seven years old; Heindrik would have been five on July 10; and little Adriaantje had been only twenty-nine months old. Now nine-year-old Gerrit was the only surviving child.

My first reaction to this disaster was a mental picture of the horrible sliding of the shrouded bodies before they splashed into the sea. I shivered.

I saw Mrs. Pleuntje Klein look at the children around her. She seemed to be searching for someone. It was as if she could not believe her children were dead, and she was still looking for them. A Dutch woman, holding on to her little girl's hand, approached her and said, "It must be a comfort to you to know that your children are in heaven."

Another woman, whose hair was falling down as she ran after her two-year-old son, caught him and picked him up in her arms. Then she went to Mrs. Klein and said, "I'm sure that you will have other children."

Pleuntje Klein made no sound to indicate that she had heard them.

Then Mary approached her. In a voice not much above a whisper, she said, "My little Jan is dead. He is also buried at sea. It is so hard, isn't it?"

Pleuntje just nodded silently in the affirmative.

I talked to Peter about this. Peter—whose name was changed by the inspectors in Baltimore to one they felt was more appropriate to his new American home—wondered what was wrong with the children. His first thought concerned the medical symptoms the children had shown. Could they have been saved if they had proper medical care?

Sometimes I have been so involved with my feelings that I didn't see all the different ways to look at a situation. Was this part of growing up? Was it mature of me to think of other people's feelings? No one was really wrong, but everyone thought his view of the situation was right.

We left Baltimore aboard a smelly little train car. The coal soot was so thick that when I blew my nose, my handkerchief was black.

I was a Dutch girl who had lived in the Friesland Province of the Netherlands. I had seen land reclaimed from the North Sea—land that was perfectly flat. Further inland, there was a gradual rise in the land. But I had never seen mountains. The train cars were pulled up the steep grades by stationary engines. We stopped near the summit of a mountain for the train to take on more water and coal.

We were allowed to walk to the summit. When I climbed to the top of the mountain, I could hardly believe my eyes. I saw dirt and rocks and grass and trees arranged in such splendor. The view was both majestic and grandeur. I stood in awe as I felt something both sacred and mysterious. I felt that I was in a place so close to heaven that it was touched by God. How could my spirits feel so high and yet I feel so small. I felt like I was such an insignificant part of God's creation.

Then I thought of Kind David's Psalm 121. "I will lift up mine eyes unto the hills from whence cometh my help. My help cometh from the Lord, which made heaven and earth."

I thought of my family back in the Netherlands. When would they receive the letter that was carried on the return trip of the *Pieter Floris*? I wish I could see Teunis and Pa tell them

27

that I was alright. I wish I could see Cornelus and Nicholaas and tell them of the ocean voyage and the mountains. However, I was not too anxious to see Beatrice and receive more of the continuous scolding.

We boarded the train once again. I held my breath most of the time that the train gathered speed and descended down the mountain. It was frightening but exhilarating. too.

At last, we arrived in Columbia, Pennsylvania, where we were packed into canal boats. I had sailed on canal boats at home and thought were a pleasant form of travel between the meadows and fields of our beautiful country.

But this was nothing like home. We were packed like herring, then portaged by means of horses and mules past Harrisburg to the mouth of the Juaniata River. Then the canal boats were lifted by locks to Hollidaysburg. Then we traveled by train to Johnstown. Again we transferred to canal boats to go on to Pittsburgh. We crossed rivers on aqueducts and passed through tunneled mountains.

Surely we were almost to Pella! Then I found out that the prairies were still a long way down the Ohio River. The men also admitted finally that no one knew precisely where on the prairies Pella was to be located.

Chapter Seven:
St. Louis

The Ohio River was broader and cleaner than any river I had seen since I came to the New World. The boats traveling from Pittsburgh to St. Louis were also larger and cleaner than any we had sailed upon so far. I told Peter that I finally felt much safer.

Peter looked at me and shrugged. "We're still not really safe," he said.

"What could possibly happen to us now?" I queried.

"An Indian attack, a storm, river pirates, or we could get stuck on a sand bar. Those, of course, are just a few things that come to mind." Suddenly I didn't feel so safe anymore.

In spite of all the possible dangers, however, we had a pleasant voyage down the Ohio River, and the last of our boats arrived in St. Louis on July 6.

St. Louis had a population of about thirty thousand people. The newspaper there printed a story about the tribe of Hollanders who were currently arriving in their town. I thought it was funny that they called us "Hollanders," because our country was actually called the Netherlands. Of course, many of the people who emigrated from the Netherlands actually came from the provinces of North or South Holland, since the seaports of Amsterdam and Rotterdam were located in these provinces. The story declared that we were a people of incredible wealth. Our trunks and chests were supposed to be filled with riches greater than those of ancient Peru. The problem with this story was that it prompted the prices of food and lodgings to rise dramatically overnight.

In St. Louis, Jan found barracks in a huge warehouse that we rented with our De Vries friends and ten other families. At night when we tried to sleep, loud music came from the local dance halls and saloons. Of course, our men didn't go into them. Well, at least most of them didn't. I heard some gossip about Reuben Van Gent, who apparently went out and actually got quite drunk. He came home to our barracks singing a bawdy tune at the top of his lungs. Some of the men told him to keep quiet, but that only made him sing louder. Then one of the men hit Reuben over the head with a chair. He slept it off, but the next morning, he refused to apologize to the group and wouldn't promise never to get drunk again. So the group told him to remain in St. Louis because the Godly people going to their promised land did not want him to accompany them.

Later, I learned that Reuben's father had died on the voyage to Baltimore. But he'd just found out that the man he'd thought of as his father was really his stepfather. His mother had been married before, and Reuben was the son of her first husband. Reuben's real father had gotten drunk and was killed in an accident with his horse and carriage. Now that Reuben knew the truth, he also learned that the money set aside in the iron chest for his family's farm would go to his younger half-brother, who was now the legal heir. It made me angry when I heard someone say that Reuben was "just like his real father," and "Blood will tell." Couldn't people see how hurt Reuben was? I felt sorry for him. He was only nineteen years old, just six years older than I.

We stayed in St. Louis for several weeks while scouts went in search of a location for our new colony. The Mormons were leaving Missouri and Illinois to go to Utah, and some of our group suggested that we could buy their land. Lewis and Clark had recently explored the Northwest Territory, and people were now moving to Oregon. Texas was finally a state instead of an independent country, and it was offering free land. Rev. Van Raalte and his group of over one hundred Dutchmen were in Holland, Michigan as of February of this year, and some people suggested that we might join them.

Peter and I talked about what we had heard. Our leaders did not want to buy the Mormon town because they wanted their own place—not one known for supporting the Mormon religion. And some of the local politicians were saying that Missouri was likely to be voted a slave state soon. The Dutchmen did not believe in slavery and did not want to live in a place that allowed the institution. Our leaders also decided that the Oregon Territory was too far away. There would be mountains and deserts to cross, and it would be impossible to get there before winter. Parts of Texas had a problem finding water, and much of the free land being offered there was barren sand. Rev. Raalte's community in Michigan was built on land covered with trees that needed to be cleared for farming.

Just when our leaders were becoming discouraged, they heard talk that Iowa had just been admitted to the Union and that government land there was available at only $1.25 an acre. Iowa had rich prairie soil and was just across the Mississippi River, which we had reached when we'd come to St. Louis. So, with much prayer, five men were sent to spy out the land. Our leaders likened themselves to the Israelites spying out the land of Canaan.

The men traveled first by boat to Keokuk and then by horse and wagon to the land office in Fairfield. There they met a circuit preacher by the name of Rev. Moses Post, who led them to an area between the Skunk and the Des Moines Rivers. They purchased claims and eighteen thousand acres of land. The area included a stone quarry and two coal mines, and a third of the area was forested. There was even a road of sorts that ran north to Des Moines and southeast to Keokuk.

Not everyone decided to go to Iowa this year. Winter would be here in about ten weeks, and many felt that was not time enough to build substantial houses. The living conditions would be primitive. A few others had jobs in St. Louis and had rented nice places to live.

Of course, most of the people wanted to leave as soon as possible. My brother was one of these. As a surveyor, he was needed to measure the new land.

My brother's name had been changed from Jan to John by the inspectors after we landed in Baltimore. John liked the American version of his name. There were so many new things to get used to! Sometimes I forgot and still called him "Jan."

The trip from St. Louis to Keokuk began on a Saturday afternoon. The passengers went by steamboat. We were still traveling on Sunday, as we often had to on this pilgrimage. We still held Sunday services, of course. Dominie Scholte gave an inspiring sermon on how we were like the children of Israel ready to enter the promised land. I thought he must have been planning this sermon since before we left the Netherlands. As we waited to reach Iowa soil, I realized that I also thought of Iowa as the promised land. I was part of it. Dominie Scholte said that it was God's plan that we were to live in Iowa. Was I part of God's plan, too? What if I hadn't climbed into that trunk? What if I'd suffocated in there, or died of starvation? I asked these hard questions of John and Mary. John said we really didn't know what God's plan was for us, but he tried to reassure me that God must have wanted me there, or I never would have survived. Mary stood silently on the deck of the steamboat with tears running down her face. Why wasn't her little child a part of God's plan to enter the promised land?

It's really true that we don't think the same way God does. For instance, I would have planned for us to land in beautiful sunshine on Monday morning. Instead it was pouring down rain.

32

We must have made the strangest wagon train that ever headed west. Actually, we were heading northwest, according to John. We were following the Des Moines River to the area that lay between it and the Skunk River. At the head of our group was a beautiful black coach, pulled by two spirited horses that belonged to Dominie Scholte. Following this were horses of all sizes and shapes. Most of us could only buy what was available and what we could afford. Some people rented horses and wagons that were driven by their owners, who would then return to Keokuk as soon as they delivered their cargo. Other people bought slow, plodding oxen with the idea of using them to clear the land and plow the soil. There were even mules and donkeys. Many people walked beside the wagons in order to leave room for the household goods they had purchased in St. Louis and Keokuk.

The wagons were of every conceivable size and description. Most were open. A few had canvas over a frame. These were called by a name that was new to me—prairie schooner. Other vehicles were simple, two-wheel carts. One man even pushed a wheelbarrow. Into these wagons and coaches and carts were piled all the earthly goods of hundreds of people.

Most of the gentlemen were dressed elegantly in short velvet jackets. There were several colors, but red was the favorite. Their shoes were leather with silver buckles, and they wore silk stockings underneath their knee breeches. Many of the ladies well as well dressed as the man. Some of their dresses were very impractical, with yards and yards of material in their skirts and petticoats. It was even said that Mrs. Scholte's blue gown was from Paris. The ladies' heads were covered with caps and bonnets of all sorts, but most were white with lace or flowers attached. The less well-to-do folk in our group were more practical in their attire, using materials such as cotton or linen, which were more plain but also more durable and washable. These more practical men wore long pants, and the women's caps were white with the typical Dutch wings curving up. I saw one lady with white wings on her hat that were at least a foot long on each side. It made me wonder if she would be literally carried away if a sudden gust of wind appeared. Most of us wore wooden shoes, which kept our feet from getting wet, unless we stepped in a puddle. The children wore smaller versions of the outfits of the adults.

We all contrasted sharply to the men from Keokuk who had rented their wagons and drove their own horses. They were very practical and had not even bothered to wash their clothes in some time.

The Dutch people wondered how the men from Keokuk could be so dirty and wear clothes so coarse. But the men from Keokuk must have wondered how these Dutch gentlemen would ever be farmers. How would such "refined" people ever survive in the wilderness?

Chapter Eight:
Iowa

We traveled up the road along the Des Moines River. Sometimes it was mud, and other times it was dry but full of ruts. Some children tried jumping across the sandstone outcroppings that were used as bridges. We came to our first county seat, a town named Keosaqua. It had a new court house. When Iowa became a state, the land was divided into one hundred counties. Each county was about twenty-five miles square, with each county seat founded in the center of the county. That way, a farmer could travel to the county seat in one day. Some of our group stayed in the new hotel built by Edwin Manning, but Mary and I slept in the wagon while John slept under it.

Ottumwa was also a county seat. People moved there after the 1843 land rush. Eddyville was another small town we passed through. People would come to greet us as they saw us pass. Sometimes they knew we were coming and had cooked or baked food to sell us.

We were only about seventeen miles from Pella when we got to Oskaloosa. This town had been founded by Daniel Boone's nephew, Captain Nathan Boone. Captain Boone led the

U. S. troops into the Iowa wilderness and made a fort at the narrows between the Des Moines and Chiquaqua Rivers. This town, with the funny Indian name, had been home to many Quakers since 1843.

When we passed through, a Quaker girl about my age caught my eye. She was staring at me, so I stared back at her. We probably looked as strange to her as she did to us. I finally remembered my manners and wished that I could greet her, but I knew no English, and she did not speak Dutch.

I determined that I had to learn English if I was to live in this country. How could I find out what was going on if I couldn't understand the language? Even the animals around here understood English. I saw more than one Dutchman get angry with his new horse because he wouldn't move until the Dutchman remembered to use the English "Gee" and "Haw." Of course, the Keokuk men thought that this was funny and doubled over with laughter.

At last we came to Pella. I was expecting at least a little town, but all I saw was a sign that said "Pella" near one little cabin and a pile of lumber. It was August 26, 1847.

One of the first orders of business was to lay out the town in a grid pattern with lots circling out from a town square. The streets that ran east and west were called Columbus, Washington, Franklin, Liberty, Union, Independence, and Peace.

The avenues running north and south were called Entrance, Inquiry, Perseverance, Reformation, Gratitude, Experience, Patience, Confidence, Expectation, and Accomplishment. Lots were numbered, and the settlers drew lots for the location of their homes.

Some farmers were fortunate enough to acquire buildings on the thirty farmsteads that had been purchased from the American settlers. Others had to make a temporary shelter since it was already the end of August. Each immigrant had given their Dutch guilders to Dominie Scholte for the purchase of land. These were stored in the iron chest that was guarded day and night until the purchase of the ground. Now each man received the portion of land that his guilders bought. Most of the larger farms were to have a portion of woods and a portion of water along either the Skunk or the Des Moines River.

On September 12, 1847, the Clerk of Court went to Pella to conduct the ceremony during which the Dutchmen would become citizens of the United States of America. Each of the men, who were twenty-one years old and therefore had reached their majority age, raised their right arms and swore allegiance to the United States. They renounced their allegiance to King William of the Netherlands. All but two of the men were literate and could sign their own names. Those who couldn't had to sign with an X.

The first thing that needed to be done now was to build shelters for each family. We constructed sod houses by first digging a foundation about four feet deep, then covering it with planks of wood. We placed prairie grass or straw and sod over the roof to protect the house's occupants from the wind. Unfortunately, these roofs sometimes leaked water. We added a fireplace along one wall of each house, and a mud-covered chimney. All of these little houses were located northwest of the Tuttle cabin, which Rev. Scholte had purchased and now lived in. The sod houses were called "Strooijstadt," or "Strawtown." The men also built a long, low wooden building in a low spot in town as a sort of barracks. But the next thing I heard was that the fall rains had flooded the barracks, and all the beds were floating in water. Most people decided to stay in the little sod houses, I guess because a leaky roof is better than a floating bed.

All day I worked with Mary heating the water for washing the pewter dishes, making the beds, sweeping the dirt floor and doing the endless cooking and baking and cleaning. I told myself that I should be happy because it was so much easier to do these things in our home than on a ship or while traveling. But I was more depressed now than when I was coming to Pella. Then, I had a sense of adventure because I wondered what each new day would bring. Now, I just had routine activities of daily living and I knew that tomorrow would bring more of the same.

All day I could work and pretend to be my happy self. At night, my thoughts and feelings caught up with me. Sometimes I could not sleep. I just tossed and turned on the straw mattress. Other times, I did go to sleep but I had terrible dreams. I dreamed that Pa saw me returning to the Netherlands and was so angry that he beat me. Other times he refused to let me inside the house because he said that I was not his daughter. No daughter of his would ever run away from home!

The next morning, I would tell myself that my gentle Pa would never hurt me. He always let Ma do any discipline. In fact, when I was little and hurt myself, like stubbing my toe or something, he would tell me how to make it well.

"Turn around three times. Now take two steps backward and count to ten. Is your toe still hurting?"

I was so busy following his instructions that I had forgotten my toe. "No, pa. You fixed it. You can fix anything."

The sun was already up as I lay on my bed thinking about Pa. I felt so guilty for the way I left him. I missed him. He must have the letter I sent with the ship on the return trip to Amsterdam. It was too soon to get an answer. I wondered if he would ever write.

Sometimes I felt that I was above the earth on a cloud watching a small Dutch girl named Sarah Rose Spoolstra. I felt that all the changes in geography, climate, language and way of life must surely be happening to someone else. Nothing seemed the same. While traveling to Pella, each day had brought a change. Now my whole culture had changed.

The Domini told us to count our blessings. I found that I needed to gather all my impressions and thoughts and sort them into piles to make sense of the world around me. When I acknowledged my feelings, I wondered what happened to the girl who was like a cat who always landed on her feet. Where was the serendipity of Sarah Rose Spoolstra? I was longing for the red brick house with a red tiled roof and real floors. Now I was living in a sod house with a straw roof and dirt floor.

In a time of countless change, it was most important to cling to old traditions. People worried about how to do this since money was very limited. It had taken more guilders to travel here than most people had planned for. This was a special concern for parents of small children because they did not want to disappoint their children on "Sinterklaas Dag," St. Nicholas' Day in December.

December 6 was "Sinterklaas Dag" or St. Nicholas Day. This was a holiday that celebrated the Saint's birthday with parties, parades and presents. Christmas was celebrated on December 25 as a separate holiday honoring Christ's birthday. The Sinterklaas Dag was based on a story about a bishop of Myra in the 4th century A.D. named St. Nicholaas. He was the protector of the poor, and unmarried women and children. St. Nicholaas' attendant was "Zwarte Piet" or Black Peter. St. Nicholaas, or Sinterklaas, as he was also called, arrives in Holland on a big ship from Spain. Zwarte Piet leads Sinterklaas through the towns on a white horse as they visit the townspeople and give gifts. Zwarte Piet always carries a big bag in which he can put unfriendly children and take them to Spain.

On December 5, the children would place hay and carrots for the horse in their wooden shoes by the fireplace or back door. When they were asleep, Sinterklaas and Zwarte Piet came over the roofs of the houses and down the chimneys to put the presents near the fireplace. The children got their presents on the morning of the 6th, the birthday of St. Nicholaas. The gifts were for children. One year you would get a little bag of salt instead of presents. That was a sign that you were getting too old for presents from Sinterklaas. Frequently people wrote poems or notes to each other wishing them a happy Sinterklaas Dag or happy St. Nicholaas Day.

Mothers managed to get enough yarn to knit new mittens

and socks that first year, but there was precious little else to be given as gifts. Doc De Vries had someone go to Keokuk and buy sugar cones so the ladies could make sweets and peppermint sticks to give to the children. He had Peter deliver them on St. Nicholas' eve. I wrote a poem teasing Peter about being Black Peter. He teased me back by calling me "Grace."

Chapter Nine:
1848

The sky was usually blue, with big fleecy clouds floating by on a gentle breeze. The wind blew eleven months out of the year in Pella, which made it ideal for windmills. August was the only month that was practically windless, and then we couldn't depend on our windmills. But the wind returned in September, and our water mills sawed wood into planks and ground wheat and corn into flour and meal. We finally built wooden fences to keep our animals from wandering too far, and people built many more barns and sheds and fences along the road going out of town. The spring, after we arrived in Pella, the Scholtes began work on their house, and we thought they intended it to be a mansion.

Some people lived in town while their men folk drove the horses to the farms to set up their homestead. I thought that wasn't a very efficient use of time. Since people already had a shelter for themselves, many farmers spent that first summer preparing farm buildings and growing crops instead of improving the living conditions in their homes. Most people still lived in the northwest part of town, in the houses built of sod and thatch. Some made improvements to their sod houses, adding new roofs of planks with new thatch over them. Some even installed plank floors and plastered their walls and white-washed them. The little houses seemed so much brighter with white walls! Windows, of course, were few and had shutters on the inside so that people could close them against storms. Most people who built new homes that year built their kitchens as a separate building behind the main house. That lessened the dangers of kitchen fires destroying a whole house. Then, too, people wouldn't have to smell food cooking all day, and the smoke from the fires wouldn't soil their draperies. Plus, it made it so much cooler in the house in the summer not to have a constant kitchen fire in it.

The sod houses had a fireplace on one wall for both warmth and cooking. The cast iron pots and Dutch ovens were kept near the fireplace. Most people who owned a butter churn usually set it on the other side of the fireplace. A wooden table was used for eating and as a counter on which to knead bread or roll out pie dough. Most of the townspeople kept their best dishes and linens and lace curtains packed in wooden trunks or barrels, waiting for the day when the women of the home would have a "real house." It wasn't practical with dirt floors to use one's good things. Some of us took to walking indoors with our shoes on instead of leaving them off at the doorstep. But a habit is a habit. Sometimes we forgot and took off our shoes as we entered the house, just as we did in the old country. The dirt floors here in America were hard on stockings, though.

Old Mr. Van Zee had heard from someone that if you mixed blood and milk and spread it on the dirt floor, it dried to a hard, shiny surface that was easier to keep clean. So he bought a couple of hogs from Oskaloosa and tried it. He said that he needed the meat anyway, and he also had a taste for *olle bollen*, which was fried in the lard from the hogs. He didn't want anything to go to waste. As it turned out, the blood and milk mixture worked quite well. But most Dutchmen didn't have access to that much blood, and milk was put to better use in butter and cheese. There was also the problem of vacating the house for at least a couple of days to let it dry. Of course, the men were more concerned with having a shelter and a suitable fireplace for cooking and heating than they were about making the houses "nice." The men constantly reminded their women that the cabins were temporary anyway.

Deer were abundant in the woods by the rivers. Even though the Indians came and shot them with their bows and arrows, we seldom saw any of the natives. If a Dutchman ever saw one, the Indian was always moving away because he had seen the strange white man long before the white man saw him. We women were not supposed to wander off outside of town, because you never knew what an Indian might do. Of course, "nice" ladies had always been taught that they were to be chaperoned whenever they went anywhere.

Mary, John, and I seldom saw an Indian, even though we spent the summer of 1848 in a tent along the Des Moines River. John, was working there to plat a new town called Amsterdam that was being built as a river port. Flatboats went down the Des Moines River to the Mississippi River at Keokuk and on to the great city of St. Louis. Returning up the Mississippi was more difficult because the current went against you. Then you had to row the whole way. Your grain would have been unloaded in St. Louis, but you probably still had a problem with weight because of the goods you were bringing back with you to Pella. Dutchmen had always traveled by water, though, so it was natural for us to think of the river as a means of transportation.

By September, we moved back into our Strooijstadt house. The winter of 1848–49 was much more severe than our first winter. People who had cabins out on the farms were isolated for about three months that winter. Since we lived in town, we were able to gather with our neighbors to socialize. The women crocheted and knitted with the wool from Steenwyk's sheep. They also used *oches,* or scraps of material, for quilts. It was so cold that winter that the men, too, learned to crochet mittens with whatever was available. We even used candlewicking as yarn. We used anything we could find to keep our hands warm when we ventured outdoors to chop wood or to feed the animals.

It was so wonderful to feel the sun on my face in the spring of 1849. Spring flowers bloomed, and the apple trees that were planted on the east edge of town blossomed as well. By the end of May, I even found some wild strawberries that we ate on our Dutch rusk. Mary cooked some of the small strawberries into a jam. Life was so much better when I could be outdoors!

It was much easier to wash clothes outdoors where there was more room to work. In winter, we washed few clothes because it was so difficult to haul the icy water and heat it, and even then we had so little room to dry them. The clothes smelled better when they dried outdoors, too, because they didn't smell of the onions in the soup pot. We always had soup on Mondays, which was also wash day. There wasn't time to cook anything else. When the weather was nice, we built the fire outdoors under the kettle and set the tin rinse tubs in different areas depending on the way the wind was blowing, to avoid getting the smoke in anyone's eyes. Then we shaved a cake of lye soap into the boiling water. We sorted the clothes into piles, with John's white shirts that he wore Sunday and the best white things in the first batch. Then the other whites, like underwear, and then the light-colored clothes and the dark ones. In the last batch we washed the breeches and rags. We mixed flour into a bowl of cold water and then into boiling water to make starch, and we rubbed the dirty spots on a scrub board, which we were fortunate to have. Finally, we used a broom handle to remove the boiling hot clothes from the kettle and place them into the rinse water and then into the starch water. People usually hung their clothes on a rope from tree to tree, if they were fortunate to have trees. Most of the trees were down by the river, not in town, which had been prairie land. If people didn't have trees, they used a couple of sapling poles and hung their rags on a chicken fence. We always poured our rinse water on our vegetables and flowers in the garden, then used the soapy water to scrub the floors and planks. We turned the tubs upside down to drain and put on a clean apron in time for four o'clock tea time.

The women always did the washing, but the men usually built the fires under the kettles and helped to fill the tubs with water. Men and women used to have separate chores, which meant that women always did "women's work" and men did "men's work." Now the work became less defined. Everyone did what they had to do to survive. Women had to help with the physical work too, especially if they lived very far from their neighbors. Except for very few people like the Scholtes, no one had servants.

Women's clothes, at least at home, changed, too. One could not use a parasol when gathering eggs or hanging up clothes, so we became unfashionably tan. When out in the hot sun, it was very uncomfortable to wear a corset of whalebone, so many waistlines grew unfashionably large. Numerous petti-coats were too hot to wear, so we adopted plain, gathered skirts. Women still wore their Dutch hats and dresses to church, but few people wore their Paris dresses, except for Mrs. Scholte, of course. There were indeed a few ladies who sat on their posteriors and embroidered or played music, but most were real helpmates—not fashionable little dolls.

In the spring of 1849, I realized that I had outgrown my two dresses. Mary told me that I could have her dress with the pink flowers because it didn't fit her anymore. I took a closer look at her and realized that she was gaining a lot of weight. Then I realized that she was going to have a baby! How dumb could I be? I lived with her, yet I didn't really see her. I thought it was funny that she had used the dress as an excuse to tell me about her pregnancy. But I realized that well bred young ladies did not talk about having babies.

Chapter Ten:
The Forty-Niners

The summer of 1849 brought lots of visitors who traded with us for corn and wheat and other supplies as they moved along the road by the Des Moines River on their way to California. Gold had been discovered at Captain John Sutter's sawmill on the fork of the American River in California. Everyone was rushing to California to stake a claim for the gold.

Covered wagons passed through Pella almost every day. Some had six or eight or even ten yoke of oxen drawing their wagons. Others had two teams of horses or mules. The Dutch people sold supplies to the gold rush visitors. A bushel of corn sold for one dollar, as did a bushel of wheat or one hundred pounds of hay. A yoke of oxen cost fifty to fifty-five dollars. Although we were happy to sell the supplies—for money was getting scarce—we women were afraid of the forty-niners. Many smelled like they had not washed for many a day, and most of the men carried firearms and were rather coarse and disorderly. Our men were glad that we didn't speak English. That way, we couldn't understand the bad words the visitors used. Whenever we were in town shopping and saw one of them, we ladies always looked the other way.

But one day when I was in the mercantile store, I saw a man who looked vaguely familiar. He was clean, and his handlebar mustache was perfect. Then he turned and looked at me with the biggest brown eyes I'd ever seen.

"I remember you," he said in Dutch. "Aren't you the girl who was the stowaway on the *Pieter Floris?* Aren't you Sarah Spoolstra?"

I must have looked horrified at him, because he laughed. "Shush!" I said. "I don't want any more people to hear about it."

I wondered how he had heard the story and knew that I was the stowaway. Nobody had talked about it for a long time. At least, I didn't think they had.

He must have read the question on my face. "Don't you remember me? I was a passenger on the *Pieter Floris*. My name is Reuben Van Gent."

Now I knew. He was the Dutchman who'd gotten drunk in St. Louis and was banned from the colony. I looked at the floor and then at the ceiling before I dared to sneak another peek at him.

Reuben laughed and twirled his mustache. Then his face grew sober as he said, "I am on my way to California. I want to see my mother before I leave. Can you tell me where she lives?"

"She lives on Peace Street," I answered. Then I realized that he had no way of knowing where any of the streets were located. "It's not far from my brother's house," I added. Now, why had I said that? I looked down at my shoe.

"How about if I give you a ride in my wagon, and you can show me the way?"

I looked around to see if anyone was watching me, but I saw no one. It would be a stupid thing to do. Nice girls did not ride with men they hardly knew.

I looked at my shoe again.

"I won't bite," he said. "And I won't tell your story if you don't tell mine." He twirled his mustache again. He had a twinkle in his eye as he looked at me. He certainly did not look dangerous

48

to me, even though I had a funny feeling in my stomach.I thought it was good that he wanted to see his mother. I wasn't too sure that his half brother Eli wanted to see him.

"Ya," I said finally. "I'll show you the way to your mother's house." I picked up the calico sewing goods that I had already paid for and walked out the door.

Fortunately, no one saw us leave the mercantile. At least, I didn't think that anyone saw us.

On the way to Reuben's mother's house, we talked about Pella, and Reuben told me the stories he had heard about the gold in California. "I want to be rich and live in a fine house in St. Louis," he said. "Then maybe Ma will come to live with me. At least I can provide well for her." All too soon, we were at the Van Gent House.

It was a longer walk to John and Mary's house from the Van Gent's than from the mercantile. I decided not to tell John or Mary that I had seen Reuben Van Gent, but even so, I didn't have to wait long for them to learn the news on their own. In fact, John came home the next day talking about how Mrs. Van Gent was so happy to see Reuben. He'd brought her an oak armoire with drawers that moved as smooth as glass. Mrs. Van Gent had invited all the neighbors to a grand celebration on Saturday night. Mary wasn't too sure that it was proper that we go to the party, especially since she was seven months with child. But I begged her to let me go, and it was decided that Mary would stay home while John accompanied me to the celebration. John said to forgive was the Christian thing to do. Besides, he said, Mrs. Van Gent would be upset if she gave a party and no one came.

Even though I was fifteen years old, I often thought that I looked younger, perhaps because I was so small. But there wasn't much I could do to look taller, except maybe wear my hair up. But I had such a problem with my fine-textured hair falling down. The hair pins just fell out. I lost them everywhere. So, I usually just wore it braided. But for this special occasion, that used to belong to Mary. I felt quite grown up.

John was right. Mrs. Van Gent was upset because the only people who came to the party were the Dominie Van Wyk and his wife and John and I. Of course, Eli van Gent was there, too. Dinner was a disaster. There was enough food for an army. I could tell that Mrs. Van Gent was angry, but she pretended that everything was fine. She talked to Mrs. Van Wyk about fashions and the new dress that Reuben had brought her. The Dominie and John spoke to Reuben about his trip to California and what supplies he would need. Sometimes they used English words, which Reuben seemed to understand. My guess was that they spoke English when they talked about things they didn't want the ladies to understand. Reuben's brother Eli either sulked or made cow eyes at me all evening. I felt out of place, like I didn't belong. I wished that I knew what the English words meant.

Reuben did not accompany his brother or his mother to church services on Sunday. Dominie Van Wyk spoke to the congregation on the text of Luke 15:11–32. Mrs. Louise Van Dalen sat at the pew ahead of me. She waved her fancy fan in front of her perspiring face. It was no wonder she was hot. She must have worn ten layers of petticoats. She sniffed a little perfume box, then picked up her daughter's white handkerchief doll and glared at her daughter. Then she and her daughter ate peppermints. At the end of the processional, she greeted the Dominie at the door.

"It was such a good sermon on the Prodigal Son, Dominie," she said sanctimoniously. "It is good to know that God forgives us even though we have fallen."

"Ya," Dominie Van Wyk agreed. "It is also important to remember that we need to forgive each other."

She said nothing, just moved on with her nose in the air.

Chapter Eleven:
First Proposal

It was hot that first week of August, and I was trying to find a cool place to read on that Sunday afternoon. It had been a week since the dinner at the Van Gent house.

I kept thinking of Reuben. I wondered if the men from St. Louis that were part of the wagon train to California had arrived in Pella yet. Well, mostly I wondered if Reuben was on his way to new adventures.

Suddenly, I heard our dog bark. Then I saw a horse and rider approach from up the street. It was Reuben.

"How are you, little one?" he asked.

"Fine," I answered. "How are you, big man?"

Reuben laughed. There was the familiar twinkle in his eye. "Pardon me," he said. "You can't be much younger than me. You did look quite grown up at dinner."

I didn't know what to say in response. I wasn't accustomed to receiving compliments. I told him that I was only fifteen, that I was born on April 3,1834. He was already twenty-one years old, and I felt flattered to have someone think that I was older than I was.

Reuben said that he needed to rest his horse. I realized that his horse was not lathered, even though the day was warm. He probably had not ridden farther than from the Van Gent residence.

Reuben tied his horse to a tree and sat down on the ground in front of me. I was eager to hear all about St. Louis. The time flew, and he must have talked for a hour or so before he looked at his pocket watch. "I really must not be late for supper." He said. "May I call on you again?"

"I'll be working in the garden every afternoon, if it doesn't rain." I was surprised at my boldness.

"God bless you. I will pray that it does not rain." He replaced his broad-brimmed felt hat.

Mary did not work in the garden anymore. She was having trouble bending and kneeling because her unborn baby was so large. Also, it was not proper for a woman who was visibly pregnant to be seen in public, and the garden could be viewed from the street. So it had become my duty to gather the vegetables. Our main meal, dinner, was at noon. Leftovers plus new vegetables made a soup that was our usual supper in the evening, except for wash day when we had soup for dinner, too. To accommodate our needs, the garden was about three city lots in size. There were always weeds to pull or hoe. But I was never so eager to work in the garden as I was when Reuben came to visit.

Reuben came every day that week to talk to me. We talked about St. Louis and the Dutchmen we knew who were still living there. We talked about the gold rush to California and the desert that needed to be crossed to reach the golden land. We talked about European affairs, such as the overthrow of King Louis Philippe of France. The King and Queen had fled the Tuileries in 1848 and gone to England, where Queen Victoria allowed them to live in exile. Reuben said that when Louis Philippe was a prince in 1796, he had spent three years traveling in eastern America. He had visited Baltimore, Washington City, and Nashville, and had crossed the Ohio River at Maysville. It seemed strange and wonderful to know that the King had visited some of the places in my country that I had seen.

There was something different about Reuben on Friday when he stopped his horse by the potato patch where I was working. He seemed shaky. He seemed nervous. He twirled his mustache.

"Do you suppose that you could invite me to supper on Saturday night, or dinner on Sunday? No, Saturday would be better."

"Why? Don't you like talking to me here?" I was trying to find out why he was so nervous.

"Well, uh, the people have arrived whom I plan to travel with. I don't have much time. Uh…I want to do the right thing. I need to talk to your brother." This time it was he who looked at the ground.

Then he looked very seriously into my eyes. "I want you to come with me to California."

I gasped. I put my hand over my mouth. I was truly shocked.

Reuben continued. "I don't have time to court you properly. I want to marry you. Will you marry me?"

Reuben had not even kissed me. He had never so much as held my hand. Yet here he was, asking me to marry him. What a romantic idea! My heart sang. You are not ready for this! my head warned me. It was too much. I burst into tears. With my hand to my mouth, I ran into the house.

Naturally, Mary wanted to know what the problem was. In between hiccups and sobs, I told her about my visits with Reuben and his proposal.

At first, Mary just listened. Then she awkwardly hugged me. She did not tell me what I should do. Instead, she asked me. "Now what do you think you should do?"

"I'm scared. I'm not ready to get married," I admitted. "But I can't face him to tell him! Now he'll think he's not good enough for me. He really is good…I don't want to hurt him."

"But you need to talk to him, Sarah. First I'll talk to John, and he'll go to the Van Gent's house and invite Reuben to supper.

Then I'll go into the other room with John, and then you must talk to Reuben."

It happened exactly the way Mary said it would. Reuben came to supper. He looked at me and quickly looked away. Mary and John left the room after they had greeted Reuben.

"I really like you, Reuben, but—"

"I know, little one," he interrupted. "It just isn't the right time. If you came with me, I fear that you would be so lonely when I was off panning gold, away from you! There are not many good women out west. If you met them, you could not even speak to them. You do not know many English words."

That was true. Since I was from Friesland, I sometimes even had trouble understanding the dialects from the other provinces. Reuben had learned English in the two years in St. Louis, but I understood very little of the new language.

He reached for my hand with tears in his eyes. "I am leaving you now," he said. "I cannot eat supper with you. I will never forget you, little one." He kissed my hand.

"I will never forget you, either," I promised. I wondered if I would ever see him again. There were so many people I would never see again.

Chapter Twelve:
Ann

It was strange that I would meet and become such good friends with Ann Davis—or perhaps it was just meant to be. I needed a good friend at the time, and I also needed some way to learn English. Ann filled both those needs.

She was climbing into her father's phaeton carriage in front of the mercantile when I first saw her. She dropped her bag onto the boardwalk, but it didn't get dirty because of the new plank boards in front of the store. Fortunately the drawstring was secure, and the bag had not opened. I called to her in Dutch, which of course she did not understand. But my noise drew her attention, and I then pointed to her fallen bag. She said something that I didn't understand, but our body language spoke a pleasant recognition of my help and her appreciation. She looked vaguely familiar, but I couldn't remember where I might have seen her before.

I next saw Ann a couple of weeks later, sitting in the phaeton carriage in front of the mercantile. Apparently she had come to town with her father, who was nowhere in sight. Ann was holding a hurt kitten, and when I examined it more closely, I saw that it had a broken leg. I motioned for her to give me the kitten and said I would get help. She just shook her head. Our inability to communicate in a common language was frustrating to both of us.

I went to Dr. De Vries' office and asked him if he had time to help a hurt kitten. He wasn't busy, so he came with me to the mercantile. Dr. De Vries spoke to Ann in English, offering to help her kitten. He gently picked up the kitten and carried it into the mercantile, intending to speak to Ann's father. None of us would have dared take an animal into the mercantile. But no one criticized the doctor. After all, he was an adult, and a well respected doctor besides. Anyway, I trotted along behind them to see what was going to happen.

Doc poured some dark liquid over the kitten's left hind paw. When he twisted the leg to bring it into alignment, the calico kitten tried to scratch its captor and get away. Doc carefully adjusted his hold on the kitten with his left hand as his right hand held the leg. He spoke to Ann in English. She stepped forward and held the kitten while Doc bound a stick to the leg to use as a splint. Next, Doc took a long piece of cotton cloth and carefully wound it around the leg and stick. I could not understand what Doc and Ann where saying because they were speaking in English.

She must have said something to him about me, because Doc turned and noticed I was there, then introduced us. He informed me that Ann expected me at her house for tea next Tuesday at three o'clock, and that she thanked me for my help. Then Doc dismissed us rather abruptly because a man came into the office bleeding from a wound in his arm.

Mary wasn't too pleased when I told her that I was expected at the "real American's" house for tea. She was obviously not in any condition to accompany me. We didn't know how to send word that I couldn't attend. And if I did go, how would I converse when I arrived?

So I went to Doc's house after supper to ask the De Vries family what to do. I thought that maybe Mrs. De Vries would accompany me. But she didn't know any more English than I did. She was also reluctant to visit the "foreigner's house." Doc laughed and reminded her that she was the foreigner, not the Ann and the rest of the Davis family.

Doc solved the problem by telling Peter to accompany me. Peter already knew some English. He wanted to be a doctor, and all of his written examinations would likely be in English. Therefore Peter had two tutors. One taught him history, sums, and Latin, and the other taught him both written and spoken English.

But Peter was not pleased. He thought that going to tea in the afternoon was a ridiculous thing for a young man to do. Reluctantly, he got the little curricle out of the carriage house and hitched it up to his father's two black stallions. He was determined to find out how fast the little two-wheeled chaise could go.

We arrived safely, but my hair was falling down. The wind had stung my eyes, which were tearing, and I felt dusty and dirty and rumpled. Miss Davis, of course, was not dressed in her usual gray Quaker clothing. Instead, she wore a dress of blue that matched her eyes, and she didn't have a hair out of place. She was very feminine and *poised*.

Peter sat across from her making cow eyes at her the whole time. He'd look up at the ceiling, pretending not to look at Ann when in reality he could look at little else. He was clearly besotted with her, and she was enjoying the attention. I might as well have not been there for all the concern anyone else demonstrated. They talked, and I couldn't understand a single word that was said. It was so frustrating. I just looked around at the plain furniture and the clean, sparse decorations. At four o'clock, we left.

"Just what did you talk about?" I demanded.

Peter did not even seem to notice how upset I was. "She mentioned seeing us arrive when the wagon train passed their farm in 1847. They lived closer to Oskaloosa then. She asked me about where I used to live, and what I'm studying now." He sighed. "She is so beautiful, and intelligent, too," he added dreamily.

That made me angry. "I would have looked more presentable if you hadn't driven so fast!"

Peter looked as if it didn't matter what I looked like.

"I want to make a good impression, too!" I said hotly.

"If you're so concerned about your reputation, Miss Spoolstra, you had better not go riding off in wagons with strange men," Peter countered. "I saw you ride off with Reuben Van Gent."

I could not help blushing, but I still defended myself. "Who do you think you are? You're not my keeper!"

"I wish you'd tell my father that! We think of you as almost a member of the family. You've practically been my sister ever since Grace—"

I interrupted him. "I am not your sister! Maybe I shouldn't be riding with you! I have a reputation to think of, after all! Stop this buggy and let me out!"

Peter stopped the buggy, and I got out and stomped home the few remaining blocks. I was so furious!

Chapter Thirteen:
New Baby

One morning when I was outside, I thought I heard someone calling my name. But then I thought that perhaps it had just been the wind. It was the first week of September, and the winds had returned just in time for the windmills to grind the newly ripened oats and corn. I heard the sound again, and it seemed to come from far away. I ran up the hill toward the house, and I saw Mary standing outside, waving her apron. As I approached her, she clutched her abdomen and bent over.

"What is it, Mary?" I asked stupidly. I knew that something was wrong, and that it had to be the baby, but I knew that it was still too early. "What's the matter, Mary?" I cried again.

"I think that my time has come," Mary replied, biting her lips.

"But it isn't time for three weeks yet! That's why John went to Knoxville today!" I was afraid for Mary's sake and kept protesting stupidly.

"Ya? Well, tell that to the baby!" Mary declared.

She leaned on me as she walked back into the house, but she had another sharp pain before I could help her into bed. The pains were now five minutes apart. I added wood to the fireplace and put water in the kettle to boil.

Mary's voice was calm, but she couldn't hide the pain on her face as she told me to hurry and get Doc De Vries. We lived two miles from town, and it was another half mile to Doc's office.

I had never ridden Midnight, John's horse. But he had taken the other two gentler horses to pull the buggy. He was planning to pick up a rocking chair that he'd ordered from Knoxville.

"Please, God," I pleaded. "Help me to ride and get Doc."

Midnight seemed to know it was an emergency. He not only cooperated with me, he galloped over the dirt road as though he were flying.

My heart sank when I approached the De Vries house. The carriage house door was open, and I could see that Doc's buggy and horses were not inside. I ran to the house and pounded on the door to Doc's office.

Mrs. De Vries hobbled to the door. I saw that her rheumatism was acting up again, but I quickly put that thought out of my mind. I was here on a more important mission. I quickly explained that Mary was about to have her baby at any time.

"Sarah, Doc left on his house calls early today," she said worriedly. "There's a storm a-brewin'. I can feel it in my bones. I wish that I could help you, but my pony has a lame leg, and I feel so poorly that I can hardly walk. I'll tell Doc as soon as he returns." She leaned on the door frame, then closed the door after I thanked her and turned away.

What could I do? I didn't know who to ask for help. There was only one thing to do, and that was to ride back to Mary and hope and pray that Doc and John would get there soon.

I found Mary crying softly when I returned. Then another pain hit her. She moaned. I bathed her face and then put the washcloth on her forehead. "What do I do now?" I cried.

"You'll do fine, Sarah," Mary said. "Remember, I have done this before." The pains were coming about every three minutes now. "All you will have to do is catch the baby," she said with a wry smile. Imagine Mary trying to calm me down when she

60

was in all that pain!

The next thing I knew, Mary was bearing down and pushing hard. Then I saw a bit of dark hair. One more push, and the baby was born, already crying.

"Clean the baby's face and wrap him in the blanket." I didn't hear any more of what Mary said because I was overwhelmed by the most welcome sound of approaching horses.

It was Doc De Vries. I was never so happy to see anyone.

"You did just fine, little Aunt Sarah," Doc said. "I may use you to help deliver all my babies."

"Oh, could you?" I asked. I was beaming. The doctor handed me the baby as he proceeded to check on Mary.

"I think I deserve some credit in this," Mary said. We all laughed. It broke the tension for the moment.

Then we heard John's horses and buggy arrive, and Mary's husband ran into the house. His face was white because he'd seen Doc's buggy and horses outside.

"You have a fine, healthy new son and a courageous wife and sister!" Doc announced.

"Isn't it a bit unseemly for a young maiden to watch a delivery?" John asked.

"She didn't just watch. She delivered your son." Doc boasted.

"But I did the hard work," Mary said. We all laughed again. "But most of all we need to thank God that everything is fine," she added. We all solemnly agreed.

"Mary and I decided to name the baby John, which means 'Beloved of God,'" John said.

Of course, we all thought of the first little Jan who was named for his father using the Dutch "Jan" instead of the American "John" that my brother had adopted. We Dutch people often named a baby after a deceased child or other family member. It somehow seemed fitting that the first child was "'Jan"and the new baby was "John."

I was still excited when I went to bed that night. Sleep

evaded me because my spirits were so high. Few events in my life had so exhilarated me as much as this perfect new baby. He was a miracle of life and I had helped him to be born! Surely there was nothing more exciting than to help deliver babies!

Could I be a midwife? Was Doc serious when he said "May I use your help to deliver all my babies?" Maybe I could also help him with sickness and injuries! It must be the most rewarding work in the whole world to help people when they need it most. Of course, Peter helps his father and Peter plans to be a doctor. But Peter has a lot of studying to do and I might help with some of the women patients.

The problem was John. He would never allow me to help Doc. In John's viewpoint, I was just a little girl. Can you believe that he would say it was "unseemly for a young maiden to watch a delivery?" After all, he and Mary live in a small cabin with me. I do know a little about "such things." I am fifteen years old. I have even had a marriage proposal! Some women of my age are married and expecting their own child.

The next morning I went to the pump and pumped water, heated it and cooked oatmeal and fried eggs and ham for breakfast. As I served John the meal that I had prepared all by myself, I inquired about the possibility of helping Doc with his baby cases.

John coughed and sputtered into his oatmeal. "I will not have a sister of mine working outside of my home and earning her living!" He shouted. "What will people think of me? Besides, you are still a child. You are too young."

When he saw that his outburst made me cry, he used a more gentle tone. "Mary and I need you here. You can learn much about taking care of a baby. Some day, you will have children of your own and this experience with caring for little John will be very valuable."

It was a good thing that the dishes were pewter. Otherwise, I surely would have broken something when I washed them.

Chapter Fourteen:
Bible Verse Contest

The winter of 1849 to 1850 was not as harsh as the previous year, but after the freedom of being outdoors during the January thaw, we were feeling closed in. Our little house seemed so cramped. Perhaps it was the baby's things that made the cabin feel more confining.

Everyone seemed to feel it. Dominie Van Wyk thought that a contest would help cheer everyone up. What better contest than to see how many Bible verses one could recite? The contest was divided into age groups, and of course the clergy were exempt.

We used the King James version of the Bible. Each person had to know the book, chapter, and verse of the text. You supplied this list and were allowed the prompting of two words. For instance, if you wrote Psalm 23:1–6, and you couldn't remember how it started, you would be prompted by the words "The Lord." You could also be given two words in each of the following verses, 2–6. If you recited a verse incorrectly, you were told at the end of each verse that you had made a mistake. You were given one chance to say it correctly before that verse would not be counted. Of course, everyone studied the Bible for the verses they already knew, and many people looked for short verses. John 11:35 was a given because you were allowed two words of prompting, and the verse only contained the words "Jesus wept." The contest took place on the first Saturday in March.

Peter and I were finalists in the fifteen-to-twenty age group. Everyone else had left the room except for us and our prompters. I couldn't hear what Peter was saying because I was concentrating on my own recitation. I had studied so hard that I was sure I would be the winner!

I was still reciting when Peter was finished, but I could tell by the way she was fidgeting that Peter's prompter was upset about something. Finally I finished my recitation. But instead of congratulating me on my 192 verses and declaring me the winner, the two prompters held a whispered conference. Then they said they needed to speak to Dominie Van Wyk about how to count the verses in Exodus and Numbers.

Peter just sat there with a complacent look on his face.

I couldn't imagine what the conflict was. The rules were so specific. I thought they were fair. Either Peter knew the verse with only two promptings or he didn't. How could you cheat?

I soon found out. Peter had recited several verses in Exodus and Leviticus and Numbers that were identical. "And the Lord spake unto Moses saying"—that was Exodus 6:10. Peter never continued to say what God had said to Moses but went to the next identical verse, such as Exodus 13:1 and Exodus 14:1, and repeated the same words as before. The only variation was "And the Lord spake unto Moses and Aaron, saying." If Peter forgot which verses contained the reference to Aaron, they were still counted because of the two-word prompting allowance. There were over forty such verses, which gave Peter a total of 210 verses. I only had 192 verses.

Dominie said that was not the true meaning of searching the Scriptures. But since no rule said you couldn't repeat the same verse from another chapter of the Bible, Peter won the prize. It was a personal journal.

I was furious with Peter.

Mary and John felt sorry for me. They even bought me a journal of my own. But it was not the same as if I'd won it.

Chapter Fifteen:
The Flood

In the summer of 1848, we lived in a newly platted town called Amsterdam, which was located on the banks of the Des Moines River. Actually, it was my brother John who platted most of the lots in town. In 1850, the town was growing well. The new general store made it convenient to keep household supplies on hand, especially since it was only three miles from the outskirts of Pella. Besides farming the surrounding land, the main industry in Amsterdam consisted of the brick and lime kilns.

Rich people had begun to build with brick, which was much more fire resistant than the wood used to build most of our cabins. Of course, the old sod houses didn't burn well, either, but people wanted to live in dwellings that were more permanent than the sod houses.

Lime was found along the banks of the Des Moines River. It was used in mortar and plaster and added to the soil to aid in the growth of plants. Mary also put a cup a day in the holes of our outhouse. It absorbed odor well.

By 1851, A.E.D. Bousquet had invested money into flatbeds to go up and down the Des Moines River to the Mississippi

River and down to St. Louis. They planned to deliver corn and other cargo to St. Louis. Other people had dreamed of making the town a port city, which is why they named it Amsterdam, after the great port city in the Netherlands. But it was Mr. Bousquet who put money behind his ideas.

Spring planting had gone well that year, and there was the promise of a bumper corn crop. Miles of wooden fences were erected around the fields to protect the crops from the animals.

In June it rained. It rained and rained. It rained like it would never stop. John and I helped people to leave the area as quickly and safely as possible, sometimes with little more than the clothes on their backs. I stood by the muddy, rushing waters and shuddered. I watched piles of debris wash along the banks. I closed my eyes at the bloated body of a dog.

I saw a kitten caught in the limbs of a tree that rested on a roof. Then the rushing waters swept over the tree limbs, and the roof swirled out of view. I wondered if the kitten still held on or was caught in the water and dragged away.

Plans for Amsterdam were swept away in the rushing waters, along with everything else.

It was dusk when we came back to Pella. We saw the *aanspreker* in his black suit, armband, and hat. Only his gloves were white. He knocked on one door, and when the owners came to the door, he did not go inside. We stopped the wagon to hear his solemn announcement that one young woman had died in childbirth. Mrs. Van Zee was only twenty-three years old. She would be buried on Saturday.

It somehow seemed fitting to see the *aanspreker* on that day. I heard of no one who died in the flood, but it was still the death of many hopes and dreams.

Everyone left Amsterdam, and it became a ghost town. Now where would the people go? Where did they belong? And where did I belong? What work was I supposed to do? I had celebrated my sixteenth birthday two months ago. I wondered what had happened to Reuben Van Gent. If I had married him at age fifteen, I might be a mother by now. Many girls were married at fifteen or sixteen. If you were twenty-five and unmarried, you were a spinster or dried-up old maid. But I was not ready to be a mother just yet.

What was I ready for? Then it came to me. It was a plan I had thought of long ago, but I'd never done much about it. I needed to learn English in order to be a real part of this new country. Who would help me? Maybe Ann would, if I asked her. I still saw her occasionally.

I took out my journal and wrote a promise to myself that I would learn to speak and read English. I felt better when I read my promise, and I decided to ask Ann the next time I saw her.

Chapter Sixteen:
The Accident

I spent some time that summer at the Davis home. Ann's mother had died a few years ago, so she now did the housework for her father. We shared a bond because we both were motherless. Ann was glad to help me learn English in return for my company and the help that I gave her with the ironing and baking. Ann hated to heat the iron in the fireplace and iron the clothes.

Ann wrote out the proper names for the items around the house. For instance, she wrote "table" on a piece of paper and placed it on the table. When I rolled out the pie dough, she'd say "rolling out the pie dough." I was supposed to repeat what she said. Then I would go around and point to items and say what I thought the correct word was. Because her people were Quakers, she used the words "thee" and "thou." When I practiced my English on John, he laughed at my "thee" and "thou." Soon I was ready to read a book that Ann had saved from her grammar school days.

Mary did not want to learn English. Away from home, she spoke only to Dutch women or to shopkeepers who were

Dutch, so she did not see any reason to learn English. John spoke Dutch to his wife, but he was speaking more and more English to the Americans.

John thought that it was good for me to speak English to little John, too. At two years old, little John mixed the words he heard. Sometimes his mother couldn't understand him when he used an English word in a sentence.

In January of 1852, we had a very bad snowstorm. Ann was caught in it on her way home from the mercantile. The horses smelled the storm in the air and galloped very fast on the road from Pella toward Oskaloosa. Suddenly they hit a rut in the road, flipping over the sleigh. Ann was thrown into a snowbank, and the sleigh runner landed on top of her, cutting deep into her left leg.

Mr. Davis was worried about the approaching storm. He saddled up his horse and went to look for his daughter. He found Ann just a mile from their farm. She was almost frozen because the heavy fur lap robe had been thrown to the side of the road. He quickly wrapped her in the robe and placed her in front of him on the horse. He rode with her as fast as he could to Doc De Vries' house.

I was at Doc's house because I had just delivered him some eggs. I quickly made some tea to warm Ann up. Her clothes were wet, so I helped to undress her and wash her with lukewarm water. Then I dried her, and we wrapped her in warm blankets. She woke up then and started to moan. Doc gave her some laudanum for pain and questioned whether to try to save the leg, which was bleeding more freely now that she was warmed. Doc removed the blood-soaked bandage and quickly rewrapped it. He went to Mr. Davis and explained the situation to him. Mr. Davis begged Doc to save Ann's leg.

Doc straightened Ann's leg as best as he could and sewed it up. Then he placed a board under it as a splint and bandaged it. Ann was so pale in contrast to the dark blankets we had wrapped around her.

Peter went with Mr. Davis to take Ann's horses and goods home, but they turned back at the edge of town. They couldn't see their hands in front of their faces. Mr. Davis stayed with Ann in Doc's spare bedroom. John came to Doc's to see why I had not returned and stayed to help for a while. Then he took me home.

The snow stopped two days later. Mr. Davis went home to care for his animals, and Doc asked Peter to fetch me to see if I could help care for Ann. She was still in the guest room at Doc's house. Mrs. De Vries' rheumatism was so bad that she was having a difficult time doing her own housework. She could not do nursing as well.

I swallowed to keep from vomiting the first time I saw Ann's leg. It was grossly swollen, and her foot was dark and hard. She was feverish, so I immediately washed her face with cool water. When Doc asked me to stay overnight in a cot beside Ann's bed, I quickly agreed.

She slept off and on during the night. Doc got up about midnight to give her another dose of laudanum. By morning, Ann's foot was black. It smelled bad, and there was a strange, red line just below her knee. Peter rode to the Davis farm to inform Mr. Davis that Ann's leg would have to be amputated in order to save her life. I stayed behind and assisted Doc in washing the table and boiling water to clean the knife before and after the amputation. Doc carried Ann into the office where he had placed the table, and soon Peter returned to assist his father. I was not allowed in the room.

The next thing I heard were Ann's terrible screams. It was the most horrible sound I'd ever heard!

A few minutes later, they carried her back to bed. She was limp—no longer conscious. At first, I thought that she was dead, but Doc assured me she was still breathing.

Doc's face showed his concern, and Peter's face was as white as a sheet.

When Ann was settled into bed, I cleaned the office with lye soap and water. Then I stayed with Ann and bathed her face with cool water and called to Doc whenever Ann moaned and cried. Doc could only give her laudanum for her pain.

She was running a fever, and gradually the stump of her leg began to grow black. Ann was always so fastidious and clean, but the odor of her leg was terrible. Doc's only choice was to perform another operation, this time amputating Ann's leg above the knee. Her screams were as terrible as before. I was nearly overcome with pity and horror. Wasn't there some medicine that would render her unconscious before the awful operation began?

Ann was so weak that it was a miracle she survived. But gradually her stump healed. I often spoke to Peter about our patient, and he was happy that there was no pus at the end of Ann's leg. He was surprised about that and told me that some physicians even believed that in such operations patients actually needed pus in order to heal properly. But Ann was proof that a wound could heal without pus, even though her leg had been so infected. I asked Doc why there had been no pus, but he said that he didn't know. When I asked if he had done anything differently, he said that there had not been enough warm water to clean the knife, so he had poured whiskey over it.

I stayed with Ann in Doc's house for most of the winter. Mary did not need my help at home because it was winter, and John was indoors most of the day.

Doc and Mrs. De Vries treated me like a daughter. Peter treated me like a sister and a friend. But he was still besotted with Ann. Peter, Ann, and I spoke English together, and my command of the language improved rapidly as a result. I didn't want to miss anything that Peter said to Ann. I was jealous that Peter paid more attention to Ann than to me. Of course, he was constantly busy. He was still going to his tutors for classes in history and Latin and English, and he often assisted his father when he made his house calls.

Peter and his parents made plans for him to further his education. Soon he would leave for Cincinnati, Ohio, where he would attend the Electic Medical College.

Chapter Seventeen:
Typhoid Fever

After burning my hand while cooking some applesauce in the fireplace, I ran to Doc's house. Something funny was going on. Since the carriage house door was closed and the horses were visible behind the fence, you would assume that Doc was home. But all the windows and doors were closed even though it was a warm, balmy day in September, 1852. I did not expect to see Peter around since he had probably already left for Cincinnati to go to medical school. But it was surprising that he had not said farewell to me. What was going on?

I quickly raced up the steps to knock on the door when I saw the notice posted on the door. "Due to the illness of Peter De Vries, we are not accepting patients or callers." I had never seen such a notice before. Doc was always available–day or night. Peter must be terribly ill.

I ran to the mercantile. You could always find out what was happening in town at either the mercantile general store or church. My painful right hand reminded me that I could also buy some salve from the mercantile.

"May I help you, miss?"

I did not recognize the man who was acting as the store-keeper and had asked the question.

I held up my hand. "I went to see Doc, but the door was locked," I said with a quiver in my voice.

"It will heal fine, I'm sure. This is the salve that you need. Have your mother put it on for you. That will be fifteen cents."

I was angry at the store keeper for treating me like a little child, even if I am short. So I cleared my throat and said, "But what is the matter with Peter, the doctor's son?"

"He is sick. But I am sure that his father will make him well soon. Doc is a good doctor." His tone of voice dismissed me. Then he even said, "Now run along home so your mother can put the salve on your hand and don't worry your pretty little head about the doctor's son."

I thought about the nerve of him–dismissing me like that. I was so angry at the storekeeper, and also worried about Peter. My hand was swollen and red and blistered and it just plain hurt. I wiped the tears from my eyes and ran home from the store.

Mary did not know what happened to Peter either. She put salve on my hand and bandaged it. Supper was ready so we waited for John to come home. We hoped that he would have news about Peter.

During our evening meal, John explained that Peter became ill after assisting a stranger who had been traveling through Pella. The man had grown ill and had come to Dr. De Vries for help. Unfortunately, the man died, and Peter now had the same symptoms as the man. First he had fever and weakness, then he had intestinal catarrh and diarrhea and red splotches on his chest. Was this the dreaded typhoid fever that was found around the swamps in the east? Apparently it was catching, since Peter became ill after caring for the stranger. Doc would allow no one else to care for Peter, and no one was allowed to visit.

There were fewer persons in church on Sunday. People were afraid to be in crowds. No one knew who might be coming down with the dreaded disease. No one wanted to bring it home to their family. When Donnie Van Wyk prayed for the "sick among us," he included both Peter and Doc's names. After the church service, whispers were that the illness was the dreaded typhoid fever. Someone had seen a very thin Peter burning his father's soiled clothing in their yard. Peter had confirmed that his father was now ill. Ironically, the father was now the patient, and the son took care of the father.

After two weeks, Doc got better. We were all saying prayers of thanksgiving for them. Peter seemed to be fine, but it took a long time for Doc to get back his vitality. Since Doc needed Peter more than ever, he did not go to the Electic Medical College of Cincinnati, Ohio as planned.

Although we had butchered most of our chickens, we still had a few laying hens that winter. I brought some eggs to Doc's house. Peter was sitting by the fireplace reading a medical book that had belonged to his father.

"I wish that you could be a doctor like your father," I blurted. I was sorry that I said it as soon as the words left my mouth. I was sure the words would hurt Peter.

"But I will be a doctor," Peter protested. "I just have to postpone it for awhile."

"But how?" I asked. " There are no medical schools around here."

"Father has officially taken me as an apprentice. After four years of reading and apprenticeship, I can go to a medical college and take examinations. After I pass the written examination, I will appear before an examining committee and pass a whole series of practical examinations. Then I will get my certificate to become a Doctor of Medicine." Peter paused. "Or I could get part of my training as an apprentice and combine this practical knowledge with the more formal education in medical school. I might be able to get even some classes here in Pella if there is a university built." Peter sounded less sure of himself now.

"Why did you get sick? I just do not think that it is fair that you can not go to medical school now!" I blurted.

"It is God's will," Peter answered. "That is what my father says."

" And you just accept that? How can you be so calm?"

"No, I do not just accept that and I have not always been so calm. I have talked with my father about it many times. I accept what I have to and I try to change what I can. I decided not to mope around and say 'poor me' but to study all I can. If we Dutchmen had just accepted the king's decree that we could not worship God in our Reformed Church Services, we would not be living in Pella today. My father says that we must study all the changes that coming to America has caused. The we must decide what to keep as our culture and what not to keep."

"What do you mean, culture?"

"Culture is everything we have been taught and experienced. That includes traditions and morals. It even includes the language that we speak, the music that we hear and the God that we worship. Of course, it includes our Dutch history and our experiences as we traveled to this land."

"Do we just accept all of this as God's will?" I asked.

"No, God has also given us free will, We must make choices. You must decide if you want to learn to be a better cook or maybe you want to study to be a school marm or teacher. You must decide what kind of man you want to marry. You even have to decide if you want to believe in God or not and how you are going to worship Him."

"You do sound like a preacher!" I emphatically stated. "How do you know all of this?"

"My father and I have talked about this many times, especially since we both have gotten sick," Peter answered.

I wished that I could talk to my mother or father and get the answers to life's questions. But Doc really had given few answers. He just challenged Peter to think for himself and make his own choices.

The rumors continued about a possible university or college right here in Pella. The Baptists were thinking of opening it in either Oskaloosa or Pella. Some townspeople were a little worried because it was the Baptists and not the Reformed people who were developing the religious university, but Dominie Scholte and other leaders in town were very much in favor of the college. They said that we were all Americans, and all good men should work together in God's name for God's purposes. So in June of 1853, it was decided that the college would be built in Pella. It was called Central University, and in the fall of 1854, forty students were in attendance.

Oh, how I wanted to go to Central University! Girls were allowed to go if someone paid their way. But I knew there would be no money for me. What was I going to do? Was I ever going to have my own home? Was I destined to be a spinster aunt, living my whole life with my brother and his family?

It was a month past little John's birthday. He fell asleep in his chair by the fire one evening. Mary was in a delicate condition again, so it was hard for her to carry him. Of course, I didn't mind undressing him and putting him to bed. It hardly seemed possible that he could be five years old all ready. He looked so angelic as he lay sleeping. Did all children look as angelic when they were asleep?

My thoughts were going through my mind in a jumble, so I found a piece of paper and began to write a poem in English.

> *Dear little child, asleeping there*
> *What thoughts aspire thy mind?*
> *Wilt thou, with swords, thy fortune find?*
> *Or tread behind a plowshare?*
> *Will thou become earth's mighty son?*
> *Or just a common John?*
> *What will the world be like to thee?*
> *Will North and South united be?*
> *Or will they still be running races,*

Until one side has won the paces?
Will they have birthed ingenious things
Not yet in dreams today?
Will these then take their fears away?
And bring no grief, regrets?
Will beggars then begin to buy?
The morbid cease to sigh?
Child, I wish that I could tell thee
Just what the future is to be.
But God, in his great wisdom, He
Hath not revealed the future's story
That we may learn to live today
With hope to pave the future's way.

It seemed that I could not write fast enough. The words just came to me. When I finished, even I was surprised at what I had written. But I felt so good. Now if I could just practice what I believed.

Chapter Eighteen:
The Poem Found

Mary was always so organized. I was more apt to gather my stuff around me in semi-disorder. It looked messy to everyone else, but I knew where everything was.

It was a glorious day in November. The sun shone, and the sky was blue. For once, there was no snow or mud. The frost glistened on the tree branches. I knew that the sun would soon melt the frost, but for now it made the trees look like an enchanted forest. I gladly went to empty the water from the wash basin and to fetch more water for cooking and cleaning. It was Tuesday, which was our ironing and mending day. But I was in no hurry to work indoors. Even the air felt fresh and clean. I didn't want to stay cooped up inside. The house seemed so small. Reluctantly, I returned indoors to resume my chores.

I dried the dishes, my hands moving slower and slower over each one. John walked into the house announcing what a great day it was. He watched me a minute.

"You are slower than molasses in January," he said.

"She isn't looking forward to cleaning her room in the loft," Mary said.

"I can tell that we're related," John commented. "I wouldn't want to stay indoors today, either. I saw some wild geese land on the water in the river. They'll probably be over in the Klein cornfield searching for leftover kernels of corn. Why don't you see if they're still around?"

John had a twinkle in his eye. I saw the look that he gave Mary. She nodded her head at me, indicating that I should go on ahead. I wasn't sure if John wanted some privacy with Mary or what. But I didn't wait to find out.

I walked along the fence that had been erected to keep the pigs, sheep, and cows out of the cornfield. There was a late-born calf following its mother while she tried to eat the grass that grew in the fence line. I didn't see any other animals. Then I sat on the grass on the hillside and dreamed about what I would do if I were grown. What did I want to be?

Mama would say that it was important to do what God wanted you to do. But how did one find out what God wanted? Did God want slaves? Would we actually have war? I thought about the 1850 Missouri Compromise, which made Missouri a slave state. Missouri was only about sixty or seventy miles away as the crow flies. There was even talk about some states in the South seceding from the Union. We Dutch people did not think slavery was moral. That was one of the reasons we didn't go to Texas for free land. Texas was a slave state. When we lived in St. Louis, the Mormons wanted to sell us their town named Navoo because they were leaving to go to Utah. If we had bought the town, we would now be living in a slave state. I thought we might still be involved with slaves, whether we wanted to or not. What would our future be? What would my future be? What did I want for me?

I really wanted to be useful like Ma would have wanted. If I had stayed in the old country, I would be a housekeeper for Pa. It was assumed that because I was a woman, I would get married and have children. What kind of house I lived in and the lifestyle I had would depend on whom I married. But what did

I want for me? One thing I knew for sure, and that was there was so much that I didn't know. I wanted to improve my reading and writing skills. My biggest dream was to study. If only I could go to the university. I so much wanted to be useful. Maybe what I wanted was to be needed. Yes, I wanted to be needed. I wanted to be needed and wanted and loved.

While I was gone, Mary decided to help me with my messy room in the loft. At least it was messy to her. While picking up my things, she noticed my poem and my journal.

Since Mary could not read English, I wasn't worried about her reading my private thoughts. But she took the poem to John, who read it and translated it for her. They also read part of my journal.

To say that I was not too happy when I returned and found that they had violated my privacy was a gross understatement. But I did not understand why Mary was crying. She wiped a tear from her eye.

"Oh, God," she prayed. "Help me to do what is right for this very precious girl who has so much talent."

How could I be angry with her when she spoke like that?

Chapter Nineteen:
De Vries Home and Garden

Mary and John's baby girl was born on November 22, 1854. Doc was with Mary for the birth of the baby this time, but I was still allowed to be in attendance. The birth was very easy this time, and Mary was in labor only six hours. The baby was very beautiful. She had lots of brown hair and looked like a little doll. My brother, John, thought that she looked like Ma, so she was named Henrietta, after our mother. Of course, Mary stayed in bed for the usual ten days, so I got to be the lady of the house.

It was fun to be in charge of the cooking. I never realized how much Mary's cooking depended on timing. I had always helped prepare food, but Mary was the one to place it in the fire and judge when it was done. She could not see the kitchen fireplace from the bedroom where she now rested, and she assumed that I had helped her enough in the past to know just how hot to make the fire. My next problem was how to maintain the heat in the correct amount to cook the food. I used the heavy pots hanging over the crane in the fireplace and the spider pots and Dutch ovens which were lying in the embers. The Dutch oven was a large pot with a channeled lid. It held live coals in the lid as well as coals beneath the oven, and the food then baked from the top as well as the bottom. To make sure that all the food was done but not overcooked in the fireplace became a test of skill and prayer.

Even though I was now twenty years old, I was not ready to be a wife and mother. There was so much I wanted to see and do and read before I settled down. A wife and mother did not have the free time that I had to read and visit with my friends.

I did not visit much with Ann that winter because she had such a hard time getting around with her peg leg and wheeled chair. About once a month or so, I brought her the *Pella Gazette,* which had been published by Dominie Scholte and Mr. E. H. Grant since February of 1855. The founding of the newspaper had been a major undertaking. The heavy press had to be hauled by wagon from Keokuk. The newspaper office was located on the corner of Main and Washington Streets.

It was after the new year of 1856 that John sat down and talked to me. He wanted to know what my plans were for the year and for my future. Apparently, my poem and what he'd read in my journal about going to the university had made an impression on him. John had never talked seriously with me before. He usually talked *to* me, not *with* me. He also teased me about being his "baby" sister. Sometimes he acted like my father because he saw himself as the patriarch of our family in America. He did love me. But he did not listen much. He mostly told me what he thought. He never thought to ask what I thought about a matter. It was as though he thought that I had no mind of my own. Of course, I had told him what I thought many times. But it was as though he were deaf if my ideas did not concur with his own. I felt that what I thought did not matter to him.

But now he asked me what I wanted to do with my life! I told him that I wanted to go to Central University. I did not have the foggiest notion of how to pay the tuition or how to pay for my keep. I also said that Ann wanted to go to Central University, too, but it was difficult to go anywhere with one leg. She stumbled often with the peg leg and had little endurance. She usually tired easily, and when she was in her wheeled chair, she couldn't push it with her hands when it got stuck in the muddy streets. The few walks around town were usually made of brick and were hard to maneuver over, since the wheels kept catching on the edge of the bricks.

I told John that I was not ready to marry. He knew that no gentleman callers were coming, so I had no prospects in sight.

Of course, there was even less room in the house now that Henrietta was walking. Then, too, I felt that I often invaded the privacy of Mary and John since I lived with them. Except at night, when they were in bed, I was always in the room with them. At night, they had the two children in the bedroom with them. Little John was big enough to sleep in the loft, but there was barely enough room for me because the walls sloped so steeply into the space.

Mary was in the room when we talked. She said little. I wondered if it was her idea that John and I have this little chat. I really felt good because John listened to me. He didn't just talk and expect me, a member of the "weaker sex," to listen. I could tell that he really thought about the questions he asked. But he didn't have any answers for me, either.

I told myself that it didn't matter that Peter had left without telling me goodbye. Even though we were only friends, I would not have taken a lengthy trip without saying goodbye to him. But I tried to convince myself that it didn't matter to me.

A couple of weeks later, John told me that he had talked to both Mr. Davis and Doc De Vries. The men had decided that if Ann and I were serious about getting a college education, they would provide it. Mr. Davis would pay for his daughter's education, and Doctor De Vries would pay for my education. In return, I would assist Mrs. De Vries around the house and Doc De Vries in the apothecary and wherever I was needed during the summer and after school hours. Mrs. De Vries now had rheumatism so bad that it was difficult for her to bend or do much work. Even needlework was difficult because her knuckles were so swollen and her fingers were so stiff. The De Vries family did have a maid who did the cleaning and another who did the cooking. The cook lived in the kitchen in a building behind the house, and the maid went home at night. Ann and I would live in Peter's room during the week. Ann would return home for the weekend while I would go home for Sunday dinner.

The De Vries home was only two years old. It was a grand house. It reminded me of a house that I had seen in St. Louis. Peter told me that it was Greek Revival in style. I didn't know much about styles, but it had a two-story porch with what Peter called Doric columns. There were two chimneys, one on each end of the house. They were so large that each of the eight rooms in the house had its own fireplace. A broad passage ran through the center of the house, with two rooms on each side. Each side had one fireplace. The four rooms upstairs were similar in size and design. The room to the left of the entrance was a combination of examining room and library for Doc's medical books. It also held Doc's desk. The right front room was a combination apothecary and waiting room. The rooms to the back were the parlor and the dinning room. The winding staircase at the end of the passage led to the upstairs rooms, three of which were bedrooms. The other was a sitting room for Mrs. De Vries. The kitchen was located in a small building behind the main house. It had two rooms, one for the cooking and one for Martha, the cook.

The house looked perfectly symmetrical from the street. There were two nine-over-nine sash windows on each side of the front door on the lower story. There were two six-over-nine windows on each side of the front door on the upper story. Around and above the front door was a two-tier, pedimented portico. Oh, it was such a grand house! It was such a pleasure to think that I would get to live there.

I moved in on April 17, 1856, just as the tulips and some of the perennials were peeping up from the ground. Peter had sent a letter to his parents, along with roots and seeds for special herbs and flowers that had potential medicinal properties. He wanted reports on how the plants had grown in the prairie ground. Doc was too busy to work in the garden. Although Mrs. De Vries loved her plants and flowers, her rheumatism made it difficult to bend her knees or move her hands to work the soil. So the task of the apothecary and herb garden became mine.

My first task was to remove the mulch from the perennials and the tulip bed very carefully so as not to disturb the root systems or bulbs. The perennials were also kept separate from the annuals in the garden because of the danger of disturbing the perennials' roots. Chamomile, comfrey, lavender, and foxglove were all perennials that were in good shape, since their roots had been established years before. The aloe vera was dead, but Mrs. De Vries had a plant in the house that had survived the winter indoors. She also grew chives indoors because she wanted the plants to mature in time for early summer salads. It took the plants four to six months to mature. Now, where was I supposed to plant the marjoram, rosemary, mint, sage, lily of the valley, pennyroyal, and chicory? I didn't know if they needed full sun or partial sun or how tall each plant would get.

In the other part of the garden, I planted dill among the beans and cucumbers and squash to keep bugs and worms off. I planted onions and garlic among the other plants—except the beans—to keep away pests. I planted tansy near the doors and windows to repel ants, flies, and mosquitoes. Since I did not know what some of the plants would look like as they were growing, I did not know if many of them were plants or weeds.

Martha, the cook, helped some in the garden, but it was Mrs. De Vries who sat in the garden, directing its care. Some of the new plants she did not know, either. We figured out that if it looked like the other plants and was growing in a row, it should not be pulled out as a weed. Martha knew what she wanted to use as herbs. But I did not have the slightest notion of their medicinal properties. Was the leaf or flower or seed or bulb to be used for medicine? Was it to be mixed with flour and the paste rolled and cut into pills, or made into a tea, or placed on the skin?

When the plants started to dry, we cut them and divided them into piles by separating each kind of plant into little bouquets. We tied them together and hung them in the kitchen on a rope to dry with the other dried herbs. What Doc did not use, we saved for seed and for Peter, whenever he came home from Cincinnati, Ohio.

Mrs. De Vries asked me to respond to Peter's letters since her rheumatism was affecting her penmanship. She gave me Peter's last two letters so I could respond properly to his questions. Of course, I read the letters that I wrote to Peter to his mother before sending them to Peter. Soon, Peter's letters arrived addressed "Dear Father, Mother, and Sarah," as though I were part of the family.

Chapter Twenty:
Smallpox

Peter wrote that he was advised to get a vaccination against the smallpox epidemic that was sweeping the country in 1856. Thousands of Indians had already died. He advised Doc to inoculate his patients against the dreaded disease. The fear was not only for the high mortality rate associated with smallpox, but its victims were often severely scarred for life.

The old name for vaccination was "variolation" because it was known for decades that the *variola* or pustular eruption from smallpox, when placed on a healthy person, usually produced only a very mild form of the disease. Edward Jenner had even used variolation with cowpox to prevent smallpox. Since cowpox was milder than smallpox, the results of the inoculation were also less severe. In 1853, a law in England required that all persons become inoculated in order to wipe out the disease. But people still feared that the inoculation might give them the disease.

Doc read Peter's letter again and decided to write to some doctors in St. Louis for the ingredients of the inoculation so that he could vaccinate those people who wanted it. He said that he wanted Mrs. De Vries to undergo the procedure but added that he'd had a mild case of pox while he was in medical school and was already immune. Doc then commented at dinner that he would ask my brother and Ann's father if they thought we should receive the inoculation.

"Excuse me," I interrupted. "Why don't you ask me? I have reached my majority age of twenty-one years, and I can think for myself." Then I smiled my sweetest smile so he would not think that I was being too impertinent.

Doc smiled back at me. "You are so little, I keep forgetting that you are grown. So, Miss Spoolstra, do you think that it is wise for you to undergo this inoculation?"

"Ya, especially since sick people keep coming here for help. One of the travelers to the West or even our own tradesmen are likely to come into contact with the disease and then come to this house for help. They said at Central that thousands of Indians have died from the disease already. But Indians are not likely to come to you for help."

Ann agreed with me. Her father said that it was all right for her to get it, but he did not want the inoculation for himself. He did not think that he would come in contact with the disease out on the farm.

Ann and I received our inoculations. All we endured from the procedure was a pustule on our arms that was mildly discomforting for about ten days. I wrote to Peter and explained my decision to receive the inoculation.

Small pox did come to Pella and to the communities surrounding it. But since word of mouth travels fast, most travelers avoided the town. The Pella Gazette published a story about the inoculations and predicted that later that fall business would pick up because the crisis of contagion would be past.

But business wasn't better in 1857. Money was scarce. People talked about the "Panic of 1857." Dominie Scholte and P. H. Bousquet and John Nollen tried to remedy the situation by forming a bank in May of 1857. They called it the Central Exchange and Land Office.

The best thing for the doldrums is a celebration. July 4, 1857 was a good day to celebrate. Not only was it the celebration of our Declaration of Independence, but it was also the summer of the tenth anniversary of our arrival in our new country.

I was one of the thirty-one young maidens chosen to represent the thirty-one states in the United States. Each of us wore white dresses with a sash bearing the name of one of the states. We all marched in the parade, which began on Washington Street.

I listened closely to the orators for any national news that might tell me what was going on in Washington City. Dominie Scholte gave a speech declaring that we must maintain our union, but little news could be garnered from such flowery praise of our country.

I looked around at the other young girls in white dresses. They were each looking to see whether any handsome young men had noticed them.

A thought suddenly hit me. I realized that I was at least three years older than all thirty of the other girls. They were all still young maidens, but I was already a spinster, an old maid.

I realized, too, that I suddenly felt old. I had never heard anyone call me an old maid to my face, but I wondered what they must have been saying behind my back. I knew that I didn't want anyone to feel sorry for me. I didn't think I could stand to pitied.

I knew I wanted to finish Central University. But I also knew that I wanted a man to love and cherish me. Was I asking too much of a man to want a husband who would be a friend and companion to me, as well as a lover? Was I setting my goals too high?

Another thing that bothered me at the festivities was how frequently Dominie Nolte and Dominie Curtis declared that our country must stay in the union. If the South secedes, as it has threatened to do, will our men here in Iowa, in Pella, go to war?

Dominie Curtis posed some interesting questions in his speech. What would a visitor from far away see in our town today? Would they see us as Americans? I thought not. We were still too Dutch. More Dutch than English was spoken on our streets, and Dutch was taught as often as English in some of our grammar schools.

I looked around at the grove that had been prepared north of town for our festivities. Banners were fluttering in the breeze. The horses in the parade were well groomed, and the carriages were well oiled and gleaming in the sunshine. The streets were only dirt, but many people had brick or plank walks. The colorful parasols matching the ladies' dresses looked like flowers in the distance.

The band was playing again, this time "The Star Spangled Banner." I studied the band members to see if there was anyone playing that I knew. A few of my classmates from Central University were there. Most of them were eighteen to twenty years old. I was already twenty-three years old.

The next order of business was dinner. I looked around for Mary and the children. As I was walking past the booths that the traders had set up to sell mementos of the occasion, I heard my name called. Looking up, I saw Doc.

"Good day Sarah, I have been looking for you," Doc said.

I wondered what case he needed my help with. I looked around to see if I could spy the patient.

Doc saw me looking around and he chuckled. "No, we do not have a patient. At least, we do not have one yet. But I do want you to do something for me."

Doc led me to an artist who was painting portraits. Most of the portraits were already partially completed. He picked up a canvas from the stack that had young girls who wore white dresses with sashes that were similar to mine. The first thing he did was to write "Alabama" on the sash in the painting. Then he filled in my features on the blank face of the portrait. The finished picture looked good. To be honest, it flattered me a bit. Doc paid the painter. I thought that he would give the picture to me but instead he held the wet portrait by the edges and said that he was going to take it home. I wondered where he would hang it.

After Doc had left. I continued on my way to find the food tables. I heard the noise of happy people before I spied the colorful tablecloths. There was such an array of food that it was a feast for the eyes. I saw fried chickens and roasted beef and hams. There were green beans and cooked red cabbage with apples. There was applesauce and many kinds of cheese. There were potato salads and creamed potatoes. The selection of breads included wheat and rye and pumpernickel. For dessert, I saw a cake with raspberries and berry and apple and pumpkin pies, and even my favorite *zoet kock,* which was something like sweet cake.

"Miss Alabama?" I heard it again. "Miss Alabama?" It took me a minute to realize that the voice was talking to me. I wore the Alabama sash, after all. I turned toward the sound and saw a woman who looked vaguely familiar to me. Then I remembered seeing her in St. Louis ten years ago. We lived in the same warehouse barracks when we were in St. Louis. Her family had decided to stay in St. Louis because her father found work and her mother wanted to stay in a "civilized" town. She had a little boy whom I guessed to be about six or seven years old, by his toothless grin. My friend was now Mrs. Nellie Johnson. She had married an American in St. Louis, but he had died in a steamboat mishap, and her parents had died of smallpox, so she decided to move to Pella to live near her brother, Frank Keppel. I promised to see her for tea some afternoon.

Now I really felt old. Here was a woman who was my age who not only had a son old enough for school, she was even a widow.

I wondered what my life would have been like if in 1849 I had married Reuben Van Gent. I might even have a six-year-old son now.

Then I saw my friend Ann. Her father was having a difficult time pushing her wheeled chair over a rut in the lawn. Her eyes brightened when she saw me. "Would you like me to get two plates of food and join you?" I asked. I was ashamed for feeling sorry for myself when Ann was cheerful in her wheeled chair. She even said she envied me when she saw me in the parade.

Chapter Twenty-One:
Medical Miracles

I received a new letter from Peter in which he wrote that this was an exciting time in medicine.

> *I'm not just interested in diagnosing a person's illness but in trying to prevent disease in the first place. That is why such things as inoculations are so important.*
>
> *We know that many diseases are catching, or "contagious," and spread by direct contact from person to person. One such disease is smallpox. Diseases are also spread by "fomes," which are inanimate things such as bedclothes. Our professors are saying that diseases are also spread by "miasmas," which are vapors in the air.*
>
> *John Snow has made studies of the number of cases of cholera in London during the epidemic in 1854. The areas around certain water supplies produced more cholera than others. A pump handle was removed from one public pump, and the number of cases of cholera in the area went down immediately. The water looked clean from this pump, but something invisible had made a difference.*

William Budd did a similar study in 1856 with the number of cases of typhoid fever in an area supplied by a water pump. Again, there was a noticeable difference in the cases of typhoid fever when people stopped using the water.

We are also studying which plants create cures for specific diseases, or at least lessen their symptoms. Our professors emphasize that we need to give some persons the medicine that we think will help them and give others an inert pill or "placebo." Time cures some symptoms, and some people will get better just because they think they will get better. We need to know which medicines really do make a difference. Also, we need to document our failures and not just our successes. Each experiment must be repeated many times by different doctors to be sure of our results.

By the way, how are the plants in the herb garden doing this year?

Sarah, you asked about the medicinal values for each plant we have planted. Here is a partial list. I will see what else I can send you.

> *Chamomile—for problems with digestion and for nervousness.*
>
> *Aloe—place the leaf on the skin for burns and for irritations.*
>
> *Peppermint—use the leaves to make a tea for heartburn and nausea.*
>
> *Lavender—used for headaches, coughs, and nervous disorders.*
>
> *Lily of the valley—for ridding the body of too much fluid and as a substitute for Digitalis, which is for the heart.*
>
> *Foxglove—used for making Digitalis.*
>
> *Sassafras—can be made into a tea and used as a blood purifier.*

I must caution you about using only very small amounts of these plants. You know that salt used in cooking can

98

enhance the flavor of foods, but too much will spoil it. It is the same with medicine, except too much may kill you. Please do not use any of these without father's approval.

Mother, you may get some relief from rheumatism by using balsam pear liniment. You make it by putting a balsam pear in a jar and covering it with spirits of turpentine. Shake once a day for two weeks. Be sure to shake it well before applying it to your swollen joints.

I know that I am repeating myself, but I want to emphasize that most medicines may do more harm than good if too much is used. Lily of the valley can be fatal if too much is used. The same amount of medicine cannot be used by everyone. Some people are much larger than others, and some people react to medicine differently than others.

Some of the fellows have gone to "ether frolics." I went to one to watch. It is a social gathering where people hold cloths with ether or nitrous gas until they feel lightheaded. If you hold it too long, you drop the cloth and pass out, or become unconscious. Some people giggle or speak in a high-pitched voice. All say they feel no pain. Some dentists are using it to extract teeth. It may be used before surgery is performed. I will never forget when Ann had her leg amputated. It would have been so much better if we could have used ether.

There is so much we know about the body, and I am learning much. But there is so much that we do not know. It seems that each question we answer inspires me to think of a hundred more questions for which we have no answer. It is exciting to be studying medicine at a time when we are learning so much!

Sarah, as an independent young woman, you may be interested in stories we hear about the suffrage movement. They are trying to get the right for women to vote. I think that it will not matter much if women vote, because they will vote as their husbands say. You are an exception, Sarah. You will vote your own mind.

99

You asked whether we hear anything about abolition.
Some men have joined the women who are suffragettes. But
I fear that we will go to war before we are rid of slavery.

These suffragettes and abolitionists march around the
government buildings holding up their signs and stopping
traffic. I wonder how much good it does. The poor fellows
who are related to them must resent the many meals that
are late and the laundry unwashed. But the newspapers
do write about them, and they are getting their message to
the people. I am happy that I live in a country where any-
one can say what they please. The freedoms of speech and
religion are very important to this Dutchman.

My candle is burning low. I must retire. Tomorrow is
a test in anatomy. I hope the good Lord keeps you well.
Sincerely,
Peter De Vries

After I read the letter, Mrs. De Vries' only comment was, "Now that he is educated, he calls us 'Mother' and 'Father' instead of 'Ma' and 'Pa.'"

I wrote a new letter to Peter and informed him that the garden was doing well, although it was not entirely symmetrical because I did not always know how tall the plants would get before I planted them. Mrs. De Vries had Martha, the cook, use the herbs in cooking. But not much was done with the plants to make medicine. Doc preferred to get his medicine from St. Louis. You could get anything in the world in St. Louis since it was such a large port city. Of course, it took about seven days to arrive.

I also told Peter that I would love to vote, but if all men were as stubborn and considered women as inferior as did the Dutchmen, then it would not happen in my lifetime.

At the home front, not much was happening. There were the usual accidents, but fortunately no epidemics. I wrote a message from Doc that he wanted to know when Peter could

100

make a trip home. He wanted Peter to bring a couple of bottles of ether with him.

Louise Van Dalen was not really Doc's favorite patient, but she was his most frequent visitor. Doc asked me to assist him with his female patients, so I got to know her well. I never could tell if she thought that she was more of a lady if she appeared wan and sickly, or if she just liked the attention. Whenever she heard that a malady was going around, she was sure that she had it. The funny thing was that she lived on Perseverance Avenue.

If Doc had more than one patient waiting, Louise Van Dalen loudly proclaimed how ill she was, and most people gladly gave up their turn for her. She would slowly rise while struggling to hold on to her parasol and her huge carpet bag. Last year, she said she had "catarrh," which is the severe inflammation of a mucus membrane that affected one's nose to the extent that one used one's handkerchief continuously. Even though I never saw her use her handkerchief, she was sure that the catarrhal was the "manifestation of some scrofulous disease which caused torpor of the liver or the want of proper excretion of the poisonous matter circulating in the blood." To have a scrofulous disease, one had to have swollen lymph nodes, which was not her problem, and she refused bloodletting or the use of leeches unless it was absolutely necessary. Well, Doc De Vries told her to drink plenty of fluids to wash out the problem. She asked if she was to get plenty of rest. Doc said that it wouldn't hurt her, and he also gave her some medicine to take. I wasn't sure what it was.

A week later, Mrs. Van Dalen's husband came to the office to ask Doc to go see her. Doc asked me to go with him to visit her. Now she complained that she was nauseous. She had stayed in bed the whole week. Doc examined her abdomen and told her to gradually build up her strength by getting up more and more each day. He also prescribed peppermint tea instead of coffee in the morning, and again in place of tea in the afternoon.

A few weeks later, a traveler from New York City brought to Pella a miracle in the form of a patent medicine. It was called

"Dr. Smith's Compound Extract of Smart-Weed." Mrs. Van Dalen bought two bottles for fifty cents each. One of the bottles she gave to Doc "in an effort to educate him in the latest of scientific matters." She kept the other bottle for her latest malady. Doc told me to read the label. It said that it was "Compounded of Smart-Weed or Water-Pepper, Jamaica Ginger, Anodyne and healing Gums, and the Best French Brandy. Taken internally, it cures Diarrhea, Dysentery (Bloody-Flux), Summer Complaint, Cholera, Cramps, and Pain in the Stomach. It breaks up Colds, Febrile, and Inflammatory Attacks, Rheumatism, and Neuralgia and relieves all Pains and Suppressions to which Females are subject from taking cold at a critical period. Taken externally, it cures Sprains and Bruises, Frost Bites, and Bites of Poisonous Insects, Caked Breast, and Enlarged Glands—in short it is an excellent Liniment for Man or Beast."

I shook my head. "Nothing can do all that!" I cried. "Can it hurt her?"

"Probably not," Doc answered, shrugging. "It may even make her feel better." With a twinkle in his eye he added, "After all, it is made with the 'Best French Brandy.'"

A month later, Mrs. Van Dalen came to Doc to announce that she was cured of cholera. No, she did not have diarrhea, but she was recovered from the "worst gastrointestinal problems." She had vomited several times a day and felt "torpor,"or lethargic, for weeks. The new medicine had apparently cured her.

A few weeks later, Mrs. Van Dalen was again a patient. Now she complained of again feeling "torpor" and "a fullness." Her breasts and glands were also sore. Doc asked me to assist him in a complete examination. He then told her that, in about six months, she would have a new addition to her family.

In due time, she was delivered of a healthy son. If you listened to Mrs. Van Dalen the next year, you would have thought she had invented motherhood, except that she would have improved on the state of pregnancy because she "suffered so."

Chapter Twenty-Two:
Wilbur

On Sundays, I usually attended church in the morning and then went home with John and Mary for Sunday dinner. I had recently seen Wilbur Klein talking to my brother after the church service but thought little about it.

Wilbur was a forty-year-old farmer whose wife had died with childbirth fever after the birth of their fifth child. His widowed mother had moved in with him to care for their little ones. I saw the oldest four children sitting in a pew at church with their father. Their grandmother stayed at home with the baby. The three little girls in their look-alike dresses reminded me of daisies. The boy, Wilbur Jr., looked like a willowy reed. He was so thin that a puff of wind could have easily blown him over. You couldn't help feeling sorry for the family. Old Mrs. Klein had aged ten years in the short time since Jeanette had died.

As usual, I went home with John and Mary for Sunday dinner. After our meal, John and little John and Henrietta went to bed for a nap. Mary sat and talked to me. We always discussed the latest ladies' news. She would have been horrified if I had called it gossip.

Today's news was that Mrs. Louise Van Dalen had gotten a new pianoforte that played psalms and hymns. Mary giggled. "Louise proudly stated that it would not play worldly music."

I thought that was strange. "How could a pianoforte know the difference?" I asked.

Mary giggled again as she quoted Louise. "The man who sold it to her demonstrated it for her. The keys wouldn't even move when he tried to play another song." Mary giggled again.

I wondered how the man who sold it to her had managed to lock the keys and unlock them without her knowing. But I figured that it wouldn't be too hard, considering how gullible Louise could be.

Mary also told me that there was talk that we might get an organ in church. But that was voted down as being too expensive by some people and too worldly by others. The voymester with his pitch pipe had to be good enough for us.

Then Mary told me her happy news that she was with child again. She was tired and wanted to rest, so I took a book and went for a walk.

When I returned, there was a carriage in the yard. I recognized it as belonging to Wilbur Klein. He and John were apparently waiting for me to return from my walk.

"I told Wilbur that you would ride with him to the evening services at church tonight," John said.

I wasn't very happy with John and Wilbur deciding what I should do, but since I could think of no reasonable objection, I went along with it.

As we rode along, we talked about the weather and Wilbur's crops. I talked about a point in Dominie Scholte's sermon, but Wilbur didn't seem to understand. He said he knew that I was going to Central University, and he told me that he'd gone to school through the fourth grade. He was proud that he could read and write Dutch but admitted that he didn't know much English. We really had very little to say to each other. I was relieved when we soon came to the church building.

104

I sat in his pew at church. Suddenly it seemed that we were a "couple." I knew that was what some of the busybodies were thinking and whispering to each other.

I went to Ann's house the next weekend, and by that time I thought that everyone would have forgotten about my attending church with Wilbur. Fat chance of that. And the following week, Wilbur just drove up to John and Mary's front door and told me we were going to church together.

In order to prevent a scene, I put on my Sunday bonnet and got into the carriage with him. Wilbur seemed relieved when I asked him to drive west toward the Des Moines River instead of to church.

He stopped the horses and allowed them to graze. "I have something that I need to talk about." He swallowed and spoke with his head down, as if he were addressing the floor of the carriage. "Miss Sarah...Oh, fiddlesticks. Miss Sarah...Shucks! What I want to say is that I want you to marry me. I have one hundred forty acres of good ground, all paid for. I can make a good living."

I looked at his balding, forty-year-old head. He certainly was not the handsome man I'd dreamed of marrying. Briefly, I wondered if this would be my last chance to marry. I certainly never intended to be a spinster. But it was 1858, and I was already twenty-four years old. But how could I marry this dullard creature who could barely read and write?

What had I done? Had I already over-educated myself to the point that no man would be a stimulating, conversational companion to me?

I closed my eyes. A memory of Peter passed through my mind. Why couldn't Wilbur be more like Peter?

I opened my eyes. Wilbur had raised his head and was regarding me. He must have seen my closed eyes and thought that I was praying.

Encouraged, he said, "Ya! I have prayed about it, too. You are the answer to my prayers."

He gave me a sincere look. Was there gratitude on his face? I felt like laughing, or crying. I truly did not want to hurt his feelings.

"Wilbur," I began. "Why do you think that I would be a good wife to you?"

He swallowed again. "Well, I have watched you. You sing pretty in church. You look like you mean the words. I think you love God…You are always so clean-looking…You don't waste money on fancy doodads…And I am lonely, and my kids need a mother." It was probably the longest speech of his life.

I repeated his words. "You want to marry me because I am pious and clean and thrifty without being frivolous. You also want a mother for your children."

Wilbur swallowed again. "Ya, you got it right."

I took a deep breath. "I am sorry, Wilbur," I said. "I just don't think—"

How could I say that he was not enough for me? Could I say that I still had dreams of being loved and cherished?

I knew I had to discourage him, so I finally mumbled that I was not ready for a house full of children. We did not go to church that evening. We sat in silence as he drove me home.

I ran into the house. I kept my composure as I explained that I wanted to go to bed early because I had a headache. After I got to bed, I cried and cried.

Why, oh why couldn't Wilbur be more like Peter? But after a few minutes of soul-searching, I finally admitted to myself that I didn't want someone *like* Peter. I wanted *Peter.*

But as the realization dawned on me, I suddenly thought of something else. I had entered this country a decade ago as Grace De Vries. Was I still Grace in the eyes of the law? Was I legally Peter's sister?

Chapter Twenty-Three:
Civil War

I finished my third year at Central in May of 1859. I was maintaining good grades, and the De Vries family was happy with me. Mary was experiencing some problems with her latest pregnancy, so I told her that I would be happy to stay with her before and after her confinement. I was sure that Doc would give me time off if I asked for it. Would she tell me when she needed me? She said that she would.

It was June 15 when I looked out the window and saw John come riding to Doc's door. He wasn't driving the wagon or buggy that he usually took to carry supplies. He was riding Midnight, his horse, and his normally ruddy face was white. Instead of his usual smile, the expression on his face was drawn.

Naturally I was afraid that something was wrong with Mary, but I had to wait until John talked to Doc before I could find out what was wrong. Didn't they know that I was an adult? I didn't want to wait a single minute.

I knocked at the door, and Doc opened it and ushered me in. John said that he had just gotten word that Pa had passed away in January.

My first reaction was relief that Mary and the babe she was carrying were both fine.

Then I realized that I would never see Pa again. I always had the fantasy that I would see him and say I was so sorry for the way I left home. Then he would forgive me and hug me and kiss me on the forehead.

John had written Pa while we were on the ship, and he'd made me write a letter, too. The letters were taken to Friesland on the return trip of our ship, the *Pieter Floris*. Beatrice had written that everyone was worried and had searched for me. Since my body was never found, they didn't know if I had drowned and had washed to sea, or had met with foul play. Pa would not hear of a funeral or memorial service for me. He said that he would not believe I was dead until he saw my body.

Of course, Pa never wrote us. I don't think he ever wrote a letter in his life. He didn't have much schooling, but he was literate. I think he was in awe of John, with his college education.

Over the years, I had dreamed that Pa would embrace me. I couldn't remember that he ever hugged me, and I couldn't remember ever seeing him embrace my mother, either. He was not a physically demonstrative person. He was a short, gentle man who never raised his voice.

Beatrice wrote once a year of any news from our province of Friesland and about the news from Driesum, the nearest town. It seemed strange that Pa died in January yet we didn't hear of it until mid-June. Of course, no ships would have sailed in the winter. The ship with our letters had landed in New York on June 1. The letter had only taken two weeks to go to Pella.

I went home with John for a few days. I cried before I went to sleep. I never saw John cry, but often his countenance was sad. I know he loved Pa, too. The only comfort was that we would see Pa and Ma in heaven because they were both Christians.

Mary and John had a son on June 26. He looked a lot like Pa. He even had a bald head. There was something about the shape of his mouth that looked like Pa, and John had inherited the same mouth and chin, so I suppose that the baby looked like both Pa and John. They named him Gerrit after Pa.

Mary had an easy birth, but she stayed in bed the customary ten days. I made the meals and cared for little John and Henrietta and the new baby. I forgot how much washing there was with a baby and small children around.

Mrs. De Vries' rheumatism grew worse, especially with the rainy days during the last of July. She fell twice, so Doc had a wheeled chair made for her. Mrs. De Vries even slept downstairs now, in a small room that Doc added the west side of the house. It looked sort of like a shed from the outside. Dr. and Mrs. De Vries needed me more and more after Mary regained her strength, so I moved back into their house. Of course, I still had my classes a few blocks away at Central University.

The students at the University were excited about the 1860 election of a new President. Of course, the women at our college would have liked to vote, but it was really not an issue. We had too much opposition from the men. Our own Dominie Scholte was a delegate from Iowa to the national convention in Chicago for the new Republican Party. He even got to meet Mr. Abraham Lincoln, for whom he voted. Mr. Lincoln asked him to come to his inauguration when he was elected. Dominie Scholte did attend the inauguration in Washington City.

The election was the last straw for the political arena in the South. In December of 1860, South Carolina seceded from the Union, and Fort Sumter was fired upon. War had begun.

In a few months, Mississippi, then Florida, Alabama, Georgia, Louisiana, and Texas joined South Carolina. The Capitol of the Confederate States of America was located in Montgomery, Alabama.

Although I had never been to Alabama, I had read as much as I could about it when I was its representative in the 1857 Fourth of July parade. I had worn the sash that read "Alabama," and I somehow felt betrayed. I couldn't imagine how people felt who lived there. They said brother was fighting brother!

By May of 1861, Virginia, Tennessee, Arkansas, and North Carolina joined the other Confederate States. The capitol was relocated to Richmond, Virginia. Would our neighbor state, Missouri, be next? It was a mere sixty to seventy-five miles as the crow flies. What about Ohio? Cincinnati was further south than much of Virginia. What about Peter?

On the twelfth of April, 1861, President Lincoln called for volunteers to fight for the Northern cause. All of the male students at Central University volunteered! Many of the young men, and even some who were married with families, crossed the Des Moines River to go to Knoxville to sign up. Our community leaders felt that it was necessary for our young men to fight. Dominie Scholte even offered a lot in town to any young man who returned from the war. In August, it would be fifteen years since we came to American to build this town. Now our young men were leaving it to fight. Some of them could not even speak English fluently.

Peter was taking his last exams to be a doctor in June of 1861. He wrote us that he was not coming home as planned. He was joining the 17th Iowa Regiment as a doctor. Many of his classmates from Cincinnati, Ohio were joining regiments as doctors. Some were joining the cause for the North, and some for the South.

I thought about joining as a nurse, but Doc said I was needed in Pella. I owed it to Doc to stay. There was only one other physician in town now that the other doctors had joined the war effort. With his increased workload, Doc needed me as a nurse and assistant more than ever. Also, his wife both wanted and needed me as well.

Chapter Twenty-Four:
Peter

I continued to write Peter whenever we had an address to which we could mail the letter.

He wrote one letter describing the countryside in Virginia and around Washington City. I thought about how dangerous it was to have the Northern capitol in Washington City and the Southern capitol in Richmond, Virginia, so close together geographically. My heart knew how dangerous it was for Peter.

I went to the post office, which was moved from West Franklin St. to the east side of the square. The square was looking more like a park now, since the cottonwood trees were growing so fast where only prairie grass grew in 1847. The square was the center of Pella, and the streets stretched out in a grid around it. The location of everything in town was told in its relationship to the square.

There was another letter from Peter. I felt like skipping and running back to the house to read it to the De Vries family.

I wanted Peter to come home soon. How long could the killing go on? It was true that the South had won a few of the first battles, but it was now 1862 and the war had gone on over a year. When the men left Pella, they had not believed that it could last more than a few months.

I wanted to belong to someone. I wanted someone to care about me. I wanted someone to know the real me. I wanted someone to talk to who would understand me. I wanted someone to laugh and cry with me. I wanted to discuss my thoughts and feelings with someone who felt the way I did. If I felt differently, it would be all right. He would never use the information to hurt me. My heart said that someone was Peter.

My heart was singing. The sunshine never looked brighter or the grass greener.

I found Mrs. De Vries in the wheeled chair in the room that had been added as a sitting room for her. It had many windows so she could sit in the sun with her indoor plants and flowers.

Dear Pa and Ma and Sarah:

I hope that this letter will not be too big a surprise for you since I have not written in three months. But here is the best news of 1862.

My heart soared! Perhaps he had some news about the war ending!

Then I read on.

I married Lucy Ann Lassiter of Raleigh, North Carolina on June 2. It is ironic that I would marry an "enemy," but I hope that I have your blessing. She is from a good family. Her parents have always been good to the Negroes who work for them on their plantation. Her personal servant is devoted to her.

Lucy came to Ohio, where her brother was a classmate of mine. She stayed with a maiden aunt, and I was introduced to her by her brother. How ironic that my Lucy Ann is married to a Northern doctor while her brother is working for the Southern cause.

Of course, we are not actually fighting. We are doctors. We care for all the sick and injured. We even care for the physical needs of the prisoners. We probably see more death and dying than most men on the battlefield. As many men die from sickness and sepsis as are killed outright. At least we now have ether and chloroform. Do you remember how awful it was to do amputations with only whiskey and laudanum? I will never forget the operation on Ann Davis.

You will love my Lucy Ann. She is beautiful. She has raven black hair and sky-blue eyes. She has the biggest smile and the littlest waist that you ever saw.

As I read the letter, clouds passed overhead and hid the sun. Then rain darkened the room. I lit the kerosene lamp, thankful for the darkness that hid my face.

This was the worst day of my life. No, the worst day was when my mother died. Pa's death and little Jan's were awful, too. But in a way, this was like a death. It was the death of my dreams.

What could I do? I didn't want to believe it. If someone else had written about it, I could have said that it wasn't true. But Peter, himself, had written the letter.

I went to my room. I said that I had a headache and didn't want to eat supper. I cried myself to sleep.

Mrs. De Vries had me write a letter to Peter telling him that they were disappointed that Peter did not marry one of his "own kind." But they wished him well and prayed that he would soon be home and would bring his new wife with him. I couldn't hide my feelings from the De Vries family, but we didn't talk about it. I hoped that they would think that I was disappointed because she was from the South.

I swore to myself that the world would never know that Peter was ever more to me than a brother or a friend.

I sometimes thought it strange that I never called Mrs. De Vries by her Christian name, but she was a very reserved person. She was like an elite, distant aunt to me, someone older that I

revered and respected but could never talk to like an equal or con-
fidante. She thought of herself as a reflection of her husband. If
you asked who she was, she would simply reply, "I am Mrs. Pieter
De Vries." She would never say that she was "Katrina De Vries."

Doc, on the other hand, was a mentor to me. He always
answered my questions honestly, never in a demeaning way. In
fact, Doc said that there was no such thing as a foolish question. I often accompanied him on his house calls. We talked a
lot on the way home. The horses seemed to know the way and
needed little guidance. I always believed that I was what Doc
wanted in a daughter. But Mrs. De Vries never really wanted
any daughter except the one who was buried at sea.

I often wondered what people wanted in a daughter. Or in a
woman. Beauty? I knew I would never be beautiful. I tried to be
clean and tidy, and I refused to fuss with furbelows or ribbons.
I didn't think that I was ugly. I just considered myself to be an
average person.

I often had reminders of what I considered my ordinariness.
One week, I went to the pottery to see about having some
replacement mugs made for Mrs. De Vries. I needed to see
Clarence, who worked in the back room. James was in the front
room where the merchandise was kept. I very politely asked to
see Clarence, who I knew from church.

James stood in the doorway and hollered. "Hey, Clarence, a
young lady wants to see you."

Clarence answered. "I'll be there in a minute. Is she good-
looking?"

James looked from my head to my feet and back up to my
head again. I blushed. James, knowing that I had heard the
exchange, answered "Not bad."

It didn't bother me so much that they looked at me like a
prize cow. What bothered me was the fact that I had made such
a neutral impression. James had not even noticed my looks
when I'd come into the store. He'd had to look again.

Chapter Twenty-Five:
Ann's Wedding

Life goes on. I lived. I worked with Doc and Mrs. Doc. I finally knew what people meant when they said, "My heart was heavy." It seemed that much of the joy I previously felt was now missing. What happened to the serendipity Sarah Rose who had a special, magical quality that found goodness without even looking for it?

I received a note from Ann. She wanted me to see her. Could I come down sometime this week? I decided it would be good to see Ann. Maybe she would cheer me up.

For once, we had no one in the waiting room, so Doc said that I could borrow the horse and buggy to go see Ann for coffee time. On the way up, I talked to myself and told myself how much I had to be thankful for. Poor little Ann with only one leg. If anyone should be despondent, it should be her. But Ann always seemed to look at the bright side of life.

I hadn't seen Ann for several months now. Since we had graduated from Central University and she didn't go to our church, I seldom saw her. I knew that she taught classes in the rural schoolhouse by the Davis farm in 1862, so she didn't come to town much. But now it was July. She would not be teaching this time of year.

One look at Ann's face made me feel better. She was so happy that she was radiant. It looked like someone had lit a candle inside her.

"Oh, Sarah, I am so happy to see ye. You. You'll help me, won't you? I want ye to stand up with me, too."

"Whoa! Ya, I'll help if I can. Now, slow down and tell me what I am to help you with."

She looked at me as if I had suddenly become an imbecile. "Why, with my wedding, of course. My note must have arrived since ye are here."

Now it was my turn to be surprised. "Your note invited me here but said nothing about a wedding. Whom are you to marry?"

Now she really looked at me as though I had suddenly lost my intelligence. "Why, Professor Stevens, of course. He came here in the spring and asked Pa if he could court me. He said he missed my smiling face," she added bashfully. "Pa was not sure at first, but Charles won him over."

Somehow, I had a hard time picturing our history professor as Ann's husband. I never dreamed of anyone calling him "Charles," unless it was his mother when he was young. Why, I thought, he must be at least forty years old! He was short and bald and rather plump.

Ann continued. "When Charles asked Pa if he could marry me, Pa said that he was happy that someone would want to marry 'his poor little cripple.' Then he had the audacity to say that he was losing a housekeeper but gaining a family. He even said that he wanted a grandson next year!" Ann blushed.

"Your Pa said that?" Would wonders never cease? It was hard to imagine staid, serious Mr. Davis talking like that.

"Ya," Ann admitted. "I listened at the door. Sarah, I want to invite all of our women classmates from Central. I know that it will be hard on some of them, with their sweethearts gone to fight in the war."

116

"Ann, I think that they'll be happy for you. Now, how can I help? It will be hard to have a grand wedding. There is such a shortage of everything. I'm surprised that you have coffee. I suppose that we could substitute molasses or sorghum for sugar in the cake. We just cannot buy anything not grown around here with the war on. What will you do for a dress? Where does the Professor's family live?"

Ann laughed at my string of questions. "Well, I got the coffee and sugar from Charles. He doesn't drink coffee but bought some before the war for his Dutch friends and students. His family is from New York. It's much too dangerous for them to travel with the war on.

"We Quakers always dress plainly. But I have a nice dress that used to belong to Mother that I can make over without too much trouble. I hated to cut into it, but under the circumstances, I'm sure she would approve. Can you help me pin it?"

I nodded. "Ann, I'm sure that we can use some flowers out of Mrs. De Vries' garden. Will you have the ceremony here in your house or at your church in Oskaloosa?"

"Charles is a Baptist, and I don't think he'd feel right about the ceremony at the Meeting House. I'm going to Pella to see about getting a room at Central for the ceremony. That will make it easier for our women friends to come, too. I will see ye when I go to Pella on Friday."

She paused for a moment, then looked at me as if she hated to ask her next question. "Sarah," she said finally, "do you suppose that the De Vries cook, Martha, would make me a cake? Or could ye, perhaps? I will provide all the ingredients, of course. I'm just afraid that if I make it, it will be crumbs by the time it rides in Pa's wagon."

"I think so. I'll certainly ask. I'll ask about the flowers, too."

Ann then asked if we had heard from Peter. I started to cry when I told her about the letter, but I felt a little relief after I confessed my feelings for him. Ann didn't know what to say. She took my hand and held it.

117

Then she said, "I feel so sad for you. So many times I wondered if I would ever marry and have a chance at having
children. Whenever I felt really sorry for myself, I remembered
the poem you wrote.

God, in His great wisdom, He
Hath not revealed the future's story
That we might learn to live today
With Hope to pave the Future's way."

Now, if only I could take my own advice.

The next day, Mrs. De Vries surprised me when I asked if I
could help Martha make the wedding cake and use some flowers from the garden.

"I'd like to help the motherless child. It will be such joy to
have a happy occasion to celebrate. I had hoped that some day it
would be Peter's wedding held here. Anyway, do you suppose
that she would consider having the wedding here? I'd like to help.
I want to attend, too, but I have such difficulty moving around."

Ann was overjoyed when I told her on Friday that Mrs. De
Vries had offered her home for the wedding. Of course Doc did
not mind. He had grown fond of Ann when she had lived there
on weekdays while in school. Besides, anything that made Mrs.
De Vries happy made Doc happy, too.

I was the bridesmaid at the Davis-Stevens wedding on
August 20. The ceremony was held in the parlor, while the cake
and coffee was served in the dining room. Professor Charles
Stevens looked a little frightened but happy and dignified.
When he stood next to Ann's wheeled chair, he did not look so
short. Ann was radiant, and I was happy for her.

Chapter Twenty-Six:
The Rebel

In the fall of 1862, I met the enemy. I learned that he was just an ordinary man.

An accident occurred just outside of Pella when a horse was spooked by some bees and reared up, flinging the driver to the ground. Then the coach rolled over the driver's right arm and leg. Both limbs were broken.

In Doc's office, I assisted Doc in holding the patient while he pulled on the leg to get it into alignment. Then Doc wrapped both limbs and bound them to boards to make them immobile. The driver was Negro. He was sweating profusely. Then he spoke in a language I could not understand.

The man sitting in a chair in the corner spoke sharply to him. "Speak English, Samson. Don't I have enough trouble without you announcing to these Yankees that we're from the low country?" Then, turning to Doc, he asked, "How soon can he take that thing off his arm and drive?"

Doc studied the splint that held the man's right elbow in extension and briefly examined the arm again. "In two or three months," he answered finally.

The well dressed man slammed his top hat against his knee and said some words that I had never heard before. They were obviously profane.

Doc stood over him and said, "Even without a lady present, I do not allow those words to be spoken in my home!" Then, turning to me, he said, "Sarah, please get us some food. I think that this gentleman would like a drink, and I want some food to go along with it. Please bring enough for me,too. We'll eat in the dining room."

The "gentleman" sat in the chair in a crumbled heap, glowering and sputtering.

I left the room to go outdoors to the kitchen and returned to the dining room with hot pea soup, slices of bread and ham, and coffee. Doc had brought a bottle of some liquor that he usually only used for medicinal purposes. Doc said that Samson could join them at the table. Samson looked bewildered, and the gentleman began sputtering again. Doc said, "Thank you, Sarah." He nodded to indicate that I was to leave the room.

Naturally I wanted to hear their conversation, but Doc would probably get more information out of them if I left the room. I went into the apothecary and waiting room, which had a fireplace in common with the dining room. The fire had died down, so I could hear quite well from my seat at the hearth.

Doc said, "I came from south Holland, which is in the Netherlands. Some people call it the 'low country.' I believe that in this country, they call the area around Charleston, South Carolina the 'low country.'"

"I live south of Charleston, Sir. I mean no harm. I just wanted to go to California to the gold fields."

"This is 1862, not 1849," Doc said with a nervous laugh.

"Don't I know it! My father threatened to disown me if I went to California in 1849. I was eighteen years old then. So I went to Yale instead. I lived in the North. I don't hate them— well, maybe I do hate the men who killed my best friend. Anyway, I came back to my plantation after a year in the war and found out

120

that my father had died and my mother had married again. My new stepfather told me to go back to Virginia. He called me a deserter. So I just took the coach and some horses and Samson and headed to California to the gold fields. I only took what was mine through inheritance. No, I am not a deserter. I only promised to fight for one year, and I gave them that year."

His words were more slurred now. Obviously he had had too much to drink.

He continued. "We cannot win this war, anyway. The North has superior railroads, supplies, and more troops. I'm not just running away. I always wanted to travel to California. But now who will drive my team? How will I get there?"

"Maybe you can learn to drive your own team, Sir," answered Doc. "But it is nearing the end of October. It is too late in the year to cross the mountains to reach California this year."

"I guess I could drive at that." He sounded as if the thought had never occurred to him. He glanced over at the man lying on the examining table. "What shall I do with Samson? He's no good to me now. Perhaps you'd buy him now, to help defer the medical expenses? I have his papers."

"My religion will not allow me to own slaves," Doc answered. "But I will take care of him until he is well. He can sleep in my bedroom. You should get a room at the hotel in town and then travel west until you get to a large city."

"Why, thank you, Sir. It has certainly been a relief to talk to a neutral person."

I wish that I could have seen the expression on Doc's face. "My only son is in the war in Virginia," Doc answered tersely. "You'd be safer if you didn't mention where you came from and if you didn't travel with a Negro. I'll take those papers for Samson now."

"Change your mind about selling him, did you?"

"No. I will give him his freedom. Under the circumstances, there will be no charge for my services. But please do not tell anyone that Samson is here."

I could hear the men moving around in the room, so I got up quickly and went upstairs.

Early the next morning, Doc asked me to come to the sun room that was now Mrs. De Vries' bedroom and sitting room. He told his wife the story of Samson and his owner. He asked that we not tell anyone that Samson was there and that I not take anyone upstairs to visit me while Samson was here.

"He sounds strong. Is he dangerous?" Mrs. De Vries queried.

"No, I don't think so. He has no weapons. He is right-handed and can't even bend his right arm. I'll explain to him that he is a free man, and I'll help him to leave when he's well enough to travel."

"How will you do this? *Why* do you do this? I still think he may be dangerous." Mrs. De Vries was clearly anxious.

"Well, my dear, do you remember hearing about the political organization called the 'Know Nothings'? I know a man who used to belong to it because he thought they were against slavery in Tennessee. But some members were actually promoting slavery. Then the gentleman became a member of the Underground Railroad. He'll help me. I won't even tell you his name, but I know I can trust him. If anyone queries us, we shall use this gentleman's words and say that we know nothing. I hide him because some men in this town have proposed a city ordinance to prohibit Negroes in the city limits after sundown. As to why I help him, read Luke 10:29 to 38."

I got my Bible out and read the story of the Good Samaritan. Of course, I was quite familiar with the story. I just didn't know that it was in the tenth chapter of Luke.

I also learned that Samson was really a humble, gentle man. He was embarrassed when I, a white woman, did anything to help him. He called me "Ma'am," and he had tears in his eyes when he told me that Doc was going to give him his freedom.

I actually missed him when he was gone.

Chapter Twenty-Seven:
1863

We received two letters from Peter in the spring of 1863. He was so tired of war. When his division in the Army moved, so did he. He usually marched about somewhere behind the center of the troops. He was never in the front lines. If they received a surprise attack from the rear, he again was not directly in the line of fire. I told myself that his goal was to get to the wounded and give them medical attention. His goal was not to kill.

He wrote that they had an epidemic of pyremia in the field hospital in Virginia. Blood letting, which was often used to lessen fevers, did nothing to help the soldiers. They were dying in greater numbers from disease than from wounds inflicted in the battlefields. Peter wrote that the odor of the suppuration was awful. They tried to isolate the men who were putrid by assigning only two men to a tent and positioning the door of the tent so the prevailing winds blew the stench away from the camp.

On a happier note, he wrote that he was going to be a father in June. He hadn't seen his wife for a couple of months, but she had written that she was well and that her family was happy about the new addition. Her brother, who had been a classmate of Peter's and also a doctor, had urged her to go to the hospital to have the baby. There they could give her chloroform to aid in the delivery. Peter had also urged her to go to the hospital, rather than to a midwife.

Then we heard nothing for months and months. The only news we had of the war came from the 17th Iowa Regiment, where most of our Pella men were. Peter was not in that division since he had joined up in Ohio.

Pella's own newspaper, *The Weekblad*, had two more deaths to report in June of 1863. They were Jacob Vogelaar, who was killed in the battle at Jackson, Mississippi, and Cornelius De Zeeuw, who died in a hospital in Keokuk, Iowa.

Sometimes we received news from *Harper's Weekly*, which was mailed to several persons in town who had subscribed. They were only too happy to share the paper with others, especially the other families with men in the army.

But still we did not hear from Peter. Finally, Doc wrote a letter himself to his commanding officer to find out if Peter was alive and well.

Then we finally received a letter from Peter.

Pa, and Ma, and Sarah,

I am well. My body is well. My heart is heavy, and my soul is in sorrow. I know that I should have written, but it was too hard to do. I must keep moving and breathing and eating to keep alive. I must survive.

My wife is dead. Now that I've written it, it still does not seem true. I blame myself. If I had not told her to go to the hospital to have the baby, she might still be alive. There was an epidemic of puerperal—childbirth fever—in the hospital. Lucy Ann died seven days later. Her autopsy showed phlebitis, lymphangitis, peritonitis, pleuitis, and meningitis. These are all infections that I believe she received because she went to the hospital. Her Aunt Edith in Cincinnati wrote me a letter informing me of Lucy's death. She told me that I should have allowed the midwife to come as Edith had suggested. She said that I was to blame. And I blame myself. If only I had not told her to go to the hospital!

But I must survive, if God is willing, to be a father to my daughter. We had agreed to name the baby Grace if it was a girl. You may think that we should have named her Lucy Ann, but she was named before we knew that my wife was to die. The child is living with Aunt Edith. I am afraid that she is telling her what a terrible father she has.

Please do not write to my Commanding Officer again! He was very upset with me for not writing to you. I promise to write more often in the future. Pray to God that this bloody war ends soon.

Love,
Peter

Peter's next letter also dwelt upon death.

Today was a very emotional day for me. As I cannot sleep, I thought that I would write and tell you about it. Today I saw two men die. Both suffered abdominal wounds from a triangular bayonet. This bayonet was out-lawed after the War of 1812 because the wounds it inflicts in the abdomen never heal—they remain open, draining wounds. After they were outlawed, some people used them as wall decorations or candle holders or such. I do not know how the bayonets came to be used again, but we have witnessed the results of their return to the battlefield. Any-way, infection around the peritoneum set in both men.

The first man to die was Joseph Smith. He cursed the South, the war, the doctors, his parents, the heat, and the pain. His soul was in torment with fear and pain. I called a clergyman to speak to him, but he cursed God and the man of God. He tossed and turned and cursed and raged.

I went to his side and asked if there was anything that I could do to help him. He cursed me again. He was still screaming when he went limp and stopped breathing.

The other man was quietly resting. His eyes also showed intense pain. When I asked what I could do to help him, he asked for a cool cloth on his face. I soaked a cloth and wiped his feverish face. I thought that I had seen him before but could not place him immediately.

He thanked me. Then he said, "I am going to die, you know. Please stay with me." I held his hand. He looked into my eyes, and seeing my sorrow, he said, "Do not grieve for me. I will be all right. Please write my mother and tell her that I am going to see my father and Jesus." He paused. I waited. I held his hand. "Tell mother that I will see her one day in heaven. Tell Eli that I love him, too."

He looked out the tent toward the open sky and smiled. Then I noticed that he was no longer breathing. It was only after he was gone that I learned his name. He was Reuben Van Gent.

I have written his mother to tell her that he is in heaven. Sarah, I know that Reuben was sweet on you a long time ago. Could you go to his mother and talk to her?

Love,
Peter

What would I say to Reuben's mother? I knew that she wanted people to think well of her son. There were some people with long memories and little forgiveness in their hearts. What she needed was people who cared about Reuben and would say they were sorry that Reuben was dead. I certainly could do that. But it wasn't easy.

I showed her Peter's letter. With her permission, I gave it to Dominie Van Wyk to use in Reuben's memorial service. I think that the letter, as well as the sermon that the Dominie preached as a result of the letter, was some comfort to Mrs. Van Gent.

Chapter Twenty-Eight:
War Ends

The Northern army had been mostly passive, setting up blockades around railroads and cities. But now the Northerners became assertive. We read in *Harper's Weekly* that General Sherman had marched to Atlanta, Georgia. He and his army lived off the land and burned what they couldn't use. Churches and private homes were all that were saved, but sometimes even they caught fire from nearby flames. Atlanta had been a major railroad and an arsenal for the Southern army. Now it was mostly ashes.

Peter couldn't tell us where he was, but he wrote a funny story about some geese who wore shoes in the Carolinas.

It seems that many Southern farmers hid their animals in the swamps to avoid having them all killed or eaten by the Northern army. One little Negro boy, about ten years old, was driving geese down a path. These geese had strange-looking feet. When we asked the boy what happened to the geese's feet, he answered, "We shoed, them, Sir." Then he explained that the geese were getting sore feet from walking so far. "So we chased them into a pan of tar, and then into a pile of sand. That's how we shoe them." Then he rolled his eyes so we couldn't see anything but the whites of his eyes. His expression was priceless. It was so funny.

In Pella, we thought that the war ended with the surrender of Robert E. Lee at the Appomattox Court House in Virginia on April 9, 1865. But that was only the surrender of part of the Southern troops. On April 13, Sherman marched into Raleigh, North Carolina.

After the war was over, Peter wrote us that he was among the troops that met at the Bennitt farmhouse on April 17, 1865 where General Joseph E. Johnston was conferring with General William T. Sherman. General Sherman rode the train from Raleigh. General Johnston rode from Greensboro. The Bennitt farm was seven miles from Durham Station, midway between the two cities. Together, they had 89,270 troops stationed in and between Raleigh and Greensboro.

But before beginning their conference, General Sherman showed General Johnston the telegram he had received announcing the assassination of President Abraham Lincoln.

They met again the next day, but the people in Washington City rejected the agreement they wrote. No one knew if the war was going to be prolonged. The stalemate went on for days.

Peter didn't dare go to visit the Lassiters, his deceased wife's family, even though he was staying near the area in which they lived. He didn't dare confer with the enemy.

The final agreement was signed at last on April 26, 1865 and included the military surrender of the Confederate troops in the Carolinas, Georgia, and Florida. Except for a few troops in Alabama and in Louisiana, the war was over. At least it was over for Peter.

Peter decided to visit the Lassiter family once the war was finally over. Their plantation was only a few miles away from

Raleigh, where he was stationed. He hoped to see Edward, but Peter didn't know how any of the Lassiter family would react to him.

Dr. Edward Lassiter arrived home only two days before Peter's visit. Edward had gotten his discharge papers in Greensboro. Lucy Ann's parents were not happy to see Peter, but they were civil to him. They inquired about the baby, but Peter really couldn't tell them much, because he had never seen her. He did inform them that he was headed north to Cincinnati, where he would get her from Aunt Edith and pay for her care. Then he planned to take baby Grace home to Pella.

Edward was more cordial than his parents. To Edward, Peter was not the enemy, he was the classmate and friend that he remembered. Except for discussing some medical procedures used during their time in the army, they wisely did not mention the war.

Edward was not one to worry about the past. Instead, he was very interested in the future. He was excited about a small book he had sent home called *The Etiology, the Concept, and the Prophylaxis of Puerperal Fever,* by Dr. Ignaz Philippe Semmelweis. Puerperal fever was commonly called childbirth fever.

Edward said that Dr. Semmelweis had written about finding little "particles" that somehow transmitted disease via the dirty hands and instruments of doctors who had just performed autopsies. He had discovered this after one of his male assistants, Kolletschka, had died from puerperal fever. Kolletschka had been nicked with a dirty scalpel while performing an autopsy on a woman who had died of childbirth fever. Professor Kolletschka had then become ill with chills and fever, and a few days later, he died. His autopsy revealed that he also had suppuration and inflammation of the lymph glands, veins, peritoneum, and meninges. These were the exact findings on the woman whose autopsy Professor Kolletschka had performed.

Dr. Semmelweis theorized that the invisible particles from the woman's autopsy had entered his friend's body through the open cut caused by the scalpel. Dr. Semmelweis also had a theory that by washing one's hands and instruments in chlorine water, doctors might reduce the number of fatalities. He then had one group wash in the chlorine water and another continue as they had always had. He then recorded the numbers of fatalities in each division of the hospital. He learned that the fatalities were indeed drastically reduced in the group that had washed in the chlorine water.

Now Dr. Lassiter was convinced that simply washing our hands and our instruments with chlorine water would reduce infection. Peter was more skeptical, but he thought it was certainly was worth a try. Peter said that he would keep records and report them by mail them to Edward.

Edward also said that a doctor named Louis Pasteur had recently proved that microorganisms were responsible for fermentation. Another man, Dr. Lister, was experimenting with the theory that the microorganisms that cause fermentation might also be causing putrefaction in wounds. Dr. Lister was using carbolic acid as an antiseptic agent.

Edward had experimental ideas of his own, including the notion that specific microorganisms might be the cause of specific diseases. Peter wrote that Dr. Edward Lassiter's excitement was contagious. "Pa," Peter wrote, "we may be on the threshold of a new medical era!"

I was excited that Peter was interested in these new theories, but I was more interested in the fact that Peter was soon coming home.

At last Peter crossed the mountains around Asheville, North Carolina and traveled up through Tennessee and Kentucky into Ohio. He picked up his daughter and boarded one steamboat bound for St. Louis, and then another one up the Mississippi River to Keokuk. Instead of the wagon train that we had formed eighteen years earlier, he rode the Des Moines Valley Railroad from Keokuk to Eddyville. Then it was only a one-day ride home to Pella on the stagecoach.

Chapter Twenty-Nine:
Peter Returns

I returned from house calls with Doc to find Peter in the the parlor. Two-year-old Grace De Vries was sitting on her grandmother's lap saying "please-no cry."

The little girl had dark hair and blue eyes. She looked like a little doll. I wanted to run and hug her.

I did not dare to look too much at Peter. I was afraid that he would read my feelings by looking at me. I had loved him for so long!

I do not remember much of what happened the next few days. Peter seemed to avoid me. Of course, there were always many people around. I knew that I would have to move out of the De Vries' house to make room for Peter and Grace. Why hadn't I moved before he came home?

Sunday came, and I went to church as usual. I wore by best blue-green dress with the very full skirt and Belgian lace at the bodice. Even though my hair was almost covered by my hat, I took special care in pinning it. The blue-green dress was a good color for my skin and hazel eyes. The matching color in my hat even brought out the red highlights in my brown hair. I knew that I looked my best. But Peter had not even awakened to come to breakfast. No one offered to walk with me to church or to drive me in the buggy. The De Vries family did not even go to church that Sunday.

As soon as the benediction was over, I climbed into the buggy to ride home with John and Mary. I did not want to stay and talk because I did not want to answer questions about Peter. If anyone asked how he was, what was I supposed to say?

After the usual chicken dinner, the Spoolstra family lay down to take their Sunday nap.

Mary and I usually did the dishes and tidied the room, But since Mary was not feeling well, I offered to do the dishes and tidy up.

My eyes were filled with tears as I contemplated my fate. Since Mary was with child again, there would soon be no room for me in their cabin. What was I going to do? Where was I going to live?

After I finished the chores, I took a book and wandered into a field to look for a shady place to read. I was crossing the road when I saw Doc's horse and buggy come up the lane. Without thinking I hurried to meet it. Someone must be very ill for Doc to see them on Sunday!

But it was Peter. "Are you coming to meet me, Miss Spool-stra?" He queried.

If he could play games, so could I. "No, sir," I answered. "I just thought that Dr. De Vries might need some help."

"I do," he answered.

"I meant the other Dr. De Vries. I suppose people will be calling him 'old Doc De Vries' now that you are home." I kept talking so Peter would not notice how nervous I was.

"Come up here and let's go look at the Des Moines river."

He held out his hand. I took it and climbed into the buggy. Peter's touch jolted me. I didn't know that I could feel like this. I also didn't know what to say.

We soon came to the Des Moines river. We rode in virtual

silence because Peter also said very little. He just stopped the buggy, climbed out, and tied the horse to a tree. Then he got a blanket and spread it on the grass. I just sat there waiting. He held his hand out to me to help me down from the buggy.

When I stood before him, he looked at me with a twinkle in his eye. "Now, Miss Spoolstra, just how do you think you can help me?"

I didn't know what to say so, I said nothing. Peter continued. "Well, let me see. I need a mother for my daughter. I need a nurse. I need a friend."

"You need my room, too!" I blurted.

"Ya, I could use that too. Of course, it was my room before it was yours."

"I'll try to find a good place to live and be a good sister to you!" I cried with tears in my eyes. Suddenly I was bawling. What on earth was wrong with me?

"Wait a minute. Are we talking about the same thing?" Peter was no longer teasing me. His face was serious; his voice concerned. " Oh, Sarah in my stupid way, I was saying that I want you at my side for life, as my wife," he said gently.

"But I'm in this country as Grace De Vries. I'm legally your sister!" I wailed.

"I talked to my father about this, Sarah. He said they don't count children under fourteen years old. You were thirteen. Doc says that your brother has your baptism certificate, so you can use that as identification. Legally you will be a citizen of the United States as my wife. Has anyone ever referred to you as Grace De Vries? What does your college diploma say?"

"My diploma says 'Sarah Rose Spoolstra.'" I answered sniffling. "Only you have ever called me Grace, when I was a little girl and you were teasing me."

"Well, you are still little but you have definitely grown up into a beautiful woman. Sarah, I wasn't ready to be married. I wanted to finish my education and become a doctor. There is only one living Grace De Vries. She is my daughter. I want her to be your daughter, too."

I sat down on the blanket and motioned for Peter to sit beside me. Since I had regained my composure, I was able to look him in the eye. I thought marriage would be a solution to Peter's problems, but would my needs be met? He had not said that he loved me. Maybe Peter still loved Lucy Ann. I needed to talk to sort things out and to find out Peter's true feelings.

"She is a special child, Peter. Her mother must have been very special, too. Tell me more about Lucy Ann."

Peter looked at me with an expression, which seemed to question: why are we talking about Lucy Ann at a time like this?

Then he looked away and softly spoke. "I did not really know her well. She was the sister of my friend and classmate, Edward Lassiter. We only kept company for a few weeks before we were wed. And then I only saw her for a total of sixteen weeks in our married life. I have known you most of my life, Sarah. I did care for her very much, but it was never like the feelings I have for you. I love you, Sarah."

At last, Peter had said the magic words, I love you. My heart beat wildly and I felt warm all over as I reached out to Peter.

He held me in his arms, but he continued talking. "Even though we were separated, I could feel close to you through your letters. I even carried that portrait of you with through the war. You wouldn't believe how many times I've spoken to that portrait."

"What portrait? Where did you get a portrait of me?'

"From Doc. I asked him to get one for me. It's the one he had painted of you on that July Fourth celebration back in 1857."

"Do you think that he knew way back then how I felt ? And how you felt?"

"Ya, I'd say he probably did." Peter moved away from me as he reached inside his coat pocket and pulled out a small jewelry box. Then Peter knelt in front of me and said, "I love you.

Please marry me."

"Ya, Peter, I love you." I opened the box to reveal an exquisite diamond ring.

"My grandfather had this diamond cut in Amsterdam for my Grandmother Anjia. I just had it placed in a new golden band for you," Peter explained.

"And during all this time I wondered if you really cared about me," I confessed. "Why didn't you ask me to marry you the day you returned home?"

"I needed some time to think about how to ask you to marry me. I was not trying to avoid you, but sometimes men like to go into a shell to think about things. Also, I wanted to talk to your brother and properly ask for your hand in marriage."

"Well, this woman feels that talking and sharing feelings and ideas helps to sort out the burdens of life. Talking creates intimacy and makes me feel better."

"I promise to talk to you, but I want to get married soon so we can share intimate ways as husband and wife."

I blushed. "Ya. Give me a few weeks for Mary and Ann to get a wedding together. Alright?"

"Ya, but don't make me wait too long. Come here my love." He held me in his arms and kissed me. I put my head on his shoulder, and I felt as though I belonged there, as if I had been waiting for this moment all my life.

"You know," I murmured, "I've looked for a long time for a place to belong. I think I have finally found my place in the promised land. I feel like Serendipity Sarah Rose Spoolstra!"

"But you will soon be *my* Serendipity Rose De Vries!"

"And my place is by your side in this new country."

"Ya," Peter answered. " By my side."